I0451212

The Feiquon Heist

D.C.J. Wardle

Clink
Street

London | New York

Published by Clink Street Publishing 2015

Copyright © 2015

First edition.

The author asserts the moral right under the Copyright, Designs and Patents Act
1988 to be identified as the author of this work.

All rights reserved. No part of this publication may be reproduced, stored in a
retrieval system or transmitted, in any form or by any means without the prior
consent of the author, nor be otherwise circulated in any form of binding or cover
other than that with which it is published and without a similar condition being
imposed on the subsequent purchaser.

ISBN: 978-1-910782-61-3
E-Book: 978-1-910782-62-0

*"Three people, three problems, one solution.
That's why the three of us have to rob this bank.
What's more, we have to do it tonight."*

Synopsis

"Three people, three problems, one solution. That's why the three of us have to rob this bank. What's more, we have to do it tonight!"

The colossal roll of thunder that roared from the night sky, close above, shaking the floor and rattling the windows in their frames did nothing to steady Kheng's frayed nerves or suppress his increasing anxiety as he cautiously led his co-conspirators through the dark corridors of the Maklai Provincial Bank. Still, once they'd made it through to the safe room, all they had to do was take the money that they needed and make their way back out. It was a simple plan, and would solve the ever-growing burden of problems that had been forming since Old Papa Han had passed away. It had never occurred to Kheng that his co-conspirators might have some very different ideas of their own about how the robbery should eventually play out. He was even less aware that he was far from alone in his attempts to capitalise on the evolving circumstances of recent weeks.

Deciding to plan a heist of the provincial bank in a sleepy backwater town in South East Asia wasn't going to be the straightforward solution that Kheng had imagined, even if he did have the advantage of being the bank's longest-serving night guard.

Part One

1. The Bank

The three oath-bound underwear-clad conspirators cautiously made their way through the dark imposing recesses of the Maklai Provincial Bank. The weak light from the torch cast angular shadows along the walls. The ordinary became sinister, the familiar warped and distorted, angular and threatening. A fork of lightning streaked momentarily across the blackened sky. The blaze of light flashed through the open door behind them at the end of the building. For an instant the inside of the bank was brightly lit, exposing their criminality, and their fear. As quickly as it had been taken from them, the menacing darkness of the dimly torch-lit hallway returned. A colossal roll of thunder roared from the sky, close above, shaking the floor and rattling the windows in their frames. The attack on their frayed nerves increased the rapid beating of their hearts, hearts that were failing to hide the anxieties they desperately needed to suppress. There was a moment of calm. Gradually the monotonous drone of the steady rain on the roof above them and in the compound of the bank regained its place as the dominant noise that surrounded them. They let the soft familiar sound provide comfort and form part of the blanket of darkness in which they sought protection. A little of their courage returned and they cautiously resumed their journey, creeping through the still, empty corridor.

Kheng was glad that the torch light was so dim. The three of them were less likely to be seen by anyone who happened to be passing outside as they stalked their way through the bank. Similarly, the gentle drumming of the rain on the roof above and the ground outside formed a protective cloak around them. It would cover any noise they might make, but also discourage any townspeople from venturing out and, by chance, spotting their movements inside the bank. Back in the village, during his childhood, it was well known that at times of rain the likelihood of thieves roaming amongst them increased. As a boy, his grandfather had told him tales about bad men who lurked in the shadows, waiting for the storm to dull the senses of their victims and provide these bad men cover for their movements. On stormy nights, Kheng had lain on the floor in the room where he would sleep. The downpours would bombard the corrugated tin roof above while Kheng listened attentively through the din for any suspicious movement outside in the compound. It was a lesson that had served him well in the army in later years. The sound of rainfall was not only cover for thieves. Now the tables were turned as he was the one enjoying the cover that the storm provided.

The three of them moved stealthily along the main corridor. The thunder had moved on, and the barbaric cries could now be heard focusing their rage over the outskirts of town. Kheng reached the room where he knew that the main safe was located, the others were close behind him. The large wooden door was all that stood between them and the money that they were risking everything to get.

Kheng straightened himself, and turned to face the

others. Due to the clandestine nature of their mission he realised that he'd been creeping around with his back hunched, in an effort to move more sneakily. He was now becoming aware of just how unnecessary that was. It was not as if they were ducking beneath a low fence line or anything like that. Also, he was getting on a bit. Arguably he was already a bit too old to be embroiled in bank heists. He was certainly too old to be doing ones which might put his back out. The others seemed to reach a similar revelation and straightened themselves up as well. Fortunately, the investment in security cameras at the Maklai provincial branch only ran to four camera units and a computer that was set up in the manager's office. There were two security cameras outside at the front of the building to monitor the main gate and the front door. Then there were two cameras inside the main business area of the small bank, one pointing at the front door from the inside, and the other covering the cashiers' desks. There were no other cameras after that. Indeed the security of the back of the bank and the safe room was almost entirely dependent on the three aging security guards who were currently spending their evening breaking into the bank with the intent to rob it.

Kheng had been a guard at the bank for more than seven years. Ever since he was finally discharged from the army he had been faithfully serving the financial institution as a lowly night guard. In return they had provided him with a slim envelope of notes in compensation each month. He had been satisfied with that. The work was easy, it got him out of the house, and it was stress free. There was almost no crime in the rural town of Maklai. Livestock missing from the yard was not uncommon, the occasional motorbike was stolen, but this was all petty theft. Certainly no one had ever been so audacious as to rob the provincial bank. In light of Kheng's contentment with his position at the bank, it was something of a surprise, even to him, that he was the mastermind behind the robbery.

Kheng held the fading torch facing upwards in the middle of the gathering so that they could all see each other. The dim light threw shadows from beneath them and changed their appearance to become like those of the curious spirits that inhabited the darker recesses of forbidden places. Kheng addressed his co-conspirators:

"So, Mr Meebor. I've got us this far. This is the safe room."

Kheng lightly patted the wooden door with the palm of his hand so there would be no confusion.

"I guess it's time to hand over to you then, and your particular expertise."

Meebor nodded thoughtfully and looked around to study his surroundings. As had been the understanding in the earlier discussion, Meebor was to devise the second stage of the heist once Kheng had got them inside. His well-practised burglar skills would be the means to gain access to the wealth that lay in the room beyond. Meebor, feeling that the dim light from the torch aiming at the ceiling above them was insufficient to make his judgement call, took the torch from Kheng and quickly shone the light around the area to examine the options.

"Under. Over. Around. Or through. Those are the usual possibilities. Going through the door or the wall would both be unnecessarily noisy and messy. It would be difficult to cover up the damage if we're hoping to get away with this. I don't have the tools to force the lock on the door. Again, it would be difficult to cover up. 'Under' is similar. You'd be better off renting the house next door and then tunnelling under the wall and into the bank, which is a big undertaking, all things considered. Also, it's not really very necessary as we've already got ourselves inside the building. So, taking stock of the situation, 'over' is very much on the cards. We should be able to remove a few ceiling tiles and climb over this wall and into the safe room that way. The building is an old town house that the Khoyleng Bank converted to meet their needs years ago. The room was never purpose-built with security in mind. There was always war, and we had the army and our national spirit to help control any criminals. I guess when they converted the building to become a bank they assumed that the safe would perform any additional security function that might be needed. They never dreamed the money would be just lying around on the floor, ripe for the taking. I'll go and get the plastic chair from outside the back door. I can stand on it, push the ceiling tile to the side and then pull myself up into the gap above."

"Make sure the chair's dry before you drag it all the way down the corridor. We don't want any drips on the floor to leave a trail for the clerk to find in the morning."

Meebor made a 'humph' noise to indicate that there was no need to state the obvious to a former expert, and then scampered off with the torch leaving Kheng and Mr Salt to wait silently in the darkness. Time seemed to go slowly in the still and pitch black of the corridor. Kheng's heart felt like it was beating ever faster with nervous anticipation. Outside he could hear the branches of the old jackfruit tree at the back of the bank as they swayed and brushed against each other in the gathering wind. His mind wandered to the large jackfruit that was hanging precariously high up near the trunk of the tree, and wondered if this was the storm that would help it down so he could carry it back home. Was it crazy to be worrying about something petty like that when they were about to rob a bank – to be concerned with something so insignificant at such a life-changing moment? His breath seemed so much louder when there was nothing to do but try to remain silent and just listen. He tried to control it. Again it was such a strange thing to do, to consciously try to regulate your breath from normal to 'stealthy' breathing.

Kheng had been impressed by Meebor. During their usual exchanges, outside of the current secretive heist operation, Meebor had always come across as a slightly sketchy village idiot. He was not someone who exuded an aura of trust, common sense or reliability. However, now that Meebor was immersed in his area of experience and expertise, it was as if a switch had been thrown and he had been somehow transformed into a professional craftsman.

Meebor quickly returned, armed with a cheap red plastic chair.

"Don't worry, Kheng, the chair's still dry. We had to put it against the wall when we were taking the oath, so it's not been out in the rain at all."

Kheng nodded with approval. He was still a little annoyed with himself for going along with the oath. At the time he'd hoped that being sympathetic towards the impromptu call for libations would calm the nerves of his team a little. In fact, it had delayed them so that they got caught in the start of the downpour. It was for this reason that they had all left their wet clothes on the steps and were currently creeping round in nothing but their underwear and the plastic bags they'd decided to put over their hands to avoid leaving fingerprints. Kheng really hoped that forensics hadn't advanced to the point of checking footprints as well, or they would be in real trouble.

Meebor put the chair against the wall. Mr Salt held it

steady while Meebor stepped onto the seat and then tried to balance on the back of the chair. Kheng was impressed by how agile he was. Meebor was also of retirement age and beyond the years that anyone would normally be expected to perform this type of gymnastics. Balancing precariously, hoping that the old chair, brittle from years of being left outside in the sunlight, did not fail, Meebor pushed a ceiling tile to the side and hoisted himself into the ceiling cavity. Kheng and Mr Salt watched from below as Meebor's legs disappeared into the void. The light from the torch gradually reduced and eventually they were left in the unwelcoming darkness again. Kheng couldn't help but sense the irony. The chair and the torch that the guards would note down in the handover book after each shift to show their chain of responsibility were the very two things that Meebor had needed to compromise the bank's security.

"I'm in, Mr Kheng."

Meebor's strangely lit face appeared at the gap in the ceiling as he stared down at them.

"Stand on the chair, Mr Kheng, give me your hand and I'll hoist you up. It's easy enough to get back down on the other side as there's a small desk to stand on."

Kheng removed the plastic bags he had used to cover his hands, tucked them into the waistband of his underwear, and then climbed up onto the chair. Meebor removed the plastic bags from his hands as well so that the hoisting process didn't turn into a slippery fiasco. Kheng, having grabbed the free hand of Meebor, soon disappeared through the ceiling and into the room beyond. The process was then repeated to enable Mr Salt, the third member of the heist, to follow them through. Within moments, all three were standing in the safe room.

Meebor shone the torch in the eyes of the other two.

"So, what next?"

Meebor's voice sounded like that of an excited child who was receiving a long-wished for present.

"Shine the light over this way."

Kheng moved over towards the corner and gestured to where he knew the old combination lock safe was positioned, beckoning the others to follow. Piled up next to the safe was a stack of about thirty cloth bags, each the size of a 15 kilo sack of rice. Meebor pointed the torch while Kheng pulled open one of the sacks. He then peered in. Mr Salt and Mr Meebor peered as well.

Meebor was the first to sum up what the others were all thinking.

"Bloody hell!"

2. Cash

Meebor picked up the first sack.

"So, what's the plan then, Mr Kheng? I say that we get all these sacks of cash back to your house and then divide it up three ways. Or do we divide it up now? It might be best if we work in a chain to get it out of the safe room. Salt can pass it up to the ceiling, I'll move it across and you can be in the corridor to catch it. Then we divide it in the corridor. After that we can all go back to our homes with our own share."

Kheng was shocked.

"Hang on, Meebor! Who said that was the deal!"

"It's what you do at this point in a heist, Mr Kheng. I've done this on a number of occasions before, remember. I've even done quite a lot of time in prison for this sort of thing, which has also given me time to think a lot about refining the process. When you rob places, especially banks, you always try to take as much money as you possibly can, and then divide it all up equally. That's how robbing stuff works. Everyone goes away happy. It's honour amongst thieves, and all of that."

Mr Salt decided to join in:

"I thought we were just going to take what was needed. Not the whole lot. But just enough. Maybe that way they won't notice it's gone. At least they won't believe that there was a bank robbery. Not in the middle of the night. They will just look at the staff that work in the bank. The ones who would normally have access to the safe. We should think about this, Mr Meebor. I can't afford to lose my job you know. Not now."

Mr Meebor shone the torch in Mr Salt's face so he could see if the man was serious.

"What does it matter if you lose your job, Mr Salt? You'll be rich. Loaded, with more wealth than you've ever had in your entire life. Look at all of this cash. Rich doesn't do justice to quite how much you'll be rolling in. You won't need a job any more. Particularly not this low wage guarding caper."

"But my wife. She was so pleased when I got the work. It really made a difference. And now she's in hospital. I don't want to upset her. Not distress her even more than she is already."

Kheng could see a more practical perspective for Mr Salt's argument:

"Also, Meebor, if we take this much money out of the bank it'll be a national scandal. It'll be one of the biggest robberies the country of Feiquon has ever seen. They'll send in special policemen from Khoyleng to investigate. It will be the news of the province and beyond for the next year. They'll be watching everyone. It'll be impossible to get away with it. We'd need to leave the town, escape from the country. I don't know how to do that and get away with it. You need papers, visas, documents for where you run to."

Meebor dropped the sack of money back down so that it would make a frustrated thud on the floor.

"We are bank robbers, right? This is a robbery! In fact, to be more precise, this is a 'robbery in progress'. That means now is not the time to sit down and map out all of the possible future implications. This is the time where we take all the loot we can carry and get out of here as fast as we can. I'm the one with the most experience at this game. Believe me, any other course of action would be deviant from the code of being a robber."

Mr Kheng did not agree. He was not committing this act in the capacity of a normal bank robber. His calling had a higher purpose. However, clearly he'd made an oversight when initiating his first ever heist. He'd assumed everyone in the gang would be thinking in the same way as him. After all, it wasn't as though he'd come up with this plan all on his own. It could be argued, from some perspectives, that it wasn't really his idea at all. Now he realised that a key preparatory step had been missed out before he and his colleagues should have embarked on their first job. There had been a real need to reach a clear agreement on just how much they were going to steal, way before they should have even thought of breaking in. This was quite a clash of ideologies to come up now, considering how far they had already come. Clearly, the problem would need to be resolved before they could proceed any further. Indeed, the consequences of not reaching an agreement, and fairly soon, could be utterly disastrous.

3. Papa Han's Funeral

Three weeks earlier...

The firecrackers exploded into life. Several ear-rattling rockets shot up into the air, whizzing enthusiastically in all directions. Some flew skywards, some skewed sideways, some narrowly missed the heads of honoured guests. Some narrowly missed the heads of non-honoured guests. Ducking from wayward funereal fireworks was one of the great social equalisers.

Kheng had positioned himself exactly where he needed to be to view the afternoon's spectacle. This wasn't his first attendance at the funeral of a respected community member by any means, and so he knew what to expect. The elaborately tiered wooden coffin that contained the body of Old Papa Han had been positioned near the middle of the crematorium area, which was really just a big field on the outskirts of town.

Kheng had made sure that he was one of the first of the onlookers to step forward and place his lighted incense sticks on the funeral pyre. He had then retreated from the incense placing formalities to stand on a small mound of earth towards the back of the gathering crowd. This would ensure he had the best seat in the house. The other mourners solemnly added their own incense sticks to the side of the coffin to pay their respects. The monks chanted while the family members laid plank after plank against the sides of the funeral pyre to construct a great lumber-yard timber cocoon. Once the pyre was completed, a prominent monk doused the arrangement with several jerry cans of petrol to ensure the up-coming ignition designed to spirit Papa Han to his next incarnation would not suffer from any false starts. Whilst the more traditional elements of the ceremony were being played out – monks, incense, flammable liquid and that sort of thing – a couple of enthusiastic men were working diligently nearby to set up the pyrotechnics.

A wooden post had been rammed almost squarely into the ground. Strapped to the top of it in a haphazard and rather overburdening manner was a large array of firecrackers and rockets. The head monk indicated to the firework man that all was ready. Having received his cue, the man who had the great fortune to be allowed to hold his lighter to the lowest string of firecrackers performed his duty with the appropriate balance of solemnity and glee that the task called for. The gunshot-like explosions were soon accompanied by the enthusiastic swoosh of rockets taking their preferred and individualistic routes. As the penultimate rocket fired up and then shot sideways in the direction of the governor's 4x4 on the edge of the field, the upward fizzle of the lighted fuse connected with the final rocket. It was the only one on the post for which a clear direction had been assigned. Once ignited, the remaining rocket whizzed horizontally and at high speed, guided along the shoulder-height strand of metal wire to which it had patiently hung. Shortly after its guided departure it careered into a second large wooden post in the middle of the cemetery. This one was laden with even more firecrackers and rockets. The resultant firework display that erupted from the second post was even more fantastic than the first. As with the original set of explosions, a further wire-guided rocket was eventually launched. This one also followed its intended route and slammed straight into the petrol infused funeral pyre. With a final bang the coffin and planks roared into a fiery blaze and the cremation began. Old Papa Han had received the elevated pomp and ceremony that was essential for him to be reborn again in style.

Kheng smiled. It was sad to lose Old Papa Han. He was a good man. However, everybody has their time and Papa Han had led a long and respectable life. Meanwhile, with a send-off like that, with two posts laden with fire crackers, his old boss couldn't want for a better start to his next incarnation. Kheng began to wonder what form Papa Han's new life might take. Papa Han had never been one for a lot of physical activity and so that ruled out much of the usual pre-departure wish list, like a magnificent bird or a majestic tiger. These were creatures that were obliged to do a lot of exercise and put considerable effort into their daily pursuits. No, a large stoic tree in a great forest would be a fitting incarnation for a man of Papa Han's character and standing. He'd enjoy that. Looking important and not having to do very much. If it was the case that he became a mighty tree in the forest, in practical terms Papa Han would be able to replace some of the huge pile of wood that had been needed to get him on to the next cycle of life in the first place. There seemed to be a whole karma element to the tree reincarnation option as well. Deep down Papa Han had been a bit of an old rascal, so he would fit in very well with some of the more mischievous tree spirits that inhabited those darker more foreboding places in the depth of the forest.

Kheng decided that he wanted to be a bird when he came back in the next reincarnation. Nothing special. Not too colourful or imposing. He certainly did not want to become one that was big enough to be of interest to a hunter or to be considered a pest to the farmers. Just a normal bird, living each day with the freedom to fly through the upper canopy of the forest, enjoying the breeze and the delights of the freedom that having wings must bring. He'd even got his own firecrackers and rockets ready for the start of the journey, and kept them in a locked metal box underneath his stilted house. He wanted to make sure he got a good and note-worthy shove in the direction of his next life, in case such a momentous beginning to the journey loaded the deck in his favour. It would be unusual for someone of his mediocre standing to have such pomp and ceremony at a final send-off. Such pyrotechnic grandeur was usually the reserve of high up government officials. However, when he'd been in the army he'd been deployed for quite a while up near the border. During that time he'd met a foreign trader who was keen to offload a considerable quantity of black powder before returning back through the check points. It was a long while back now, but after an extensive service in the military Kheng knew about explosives and pyrotechnics reasonably well. Well enough to know that the inexpensive gun-powder in his rockets would keep for years if stored properly and would make for a fantastic funeral.

Once the fire for Papa Han's coffin was lit, and the petrol-fuelled whoosh had quickly simmered down to a burning pile of planks and lumber, the funeral ceremony was effectively over. The family and monks had been making preparations and ceremony for much of the day while the invited guests had looked on. Now the ceremony was complete. The well-wishers and mourners milled around for a short while and then gradually made their way back into town, by car, motorbike or by walking.

Kheng walked. It was a nice afternoon and he didn't have to be back at the bank for a couple of hours for his guard duty. It was a little strange thinking about going back to the bank now that Old Papa Han was on his journey in the next stage of his cycle of life. Papa Han had been at the Maklai Provincial Bank as long as Kheng could remember. In a way, Kheng thought of the bank and Old Papa Han as almost the same thing.

4. The Guard

The first rays of the sun began to glint from behind the leaves of the mango tree that grew over the wall in the garden at the side of the bank. The air felt fresh, a slight breeze began to rustle in the leaves. The gentle noise suggested that the wind would take the edge off the heat from the rising tropical sun. It was the first day that Papa Han had been truly gone from them, and it felt like a new beginning. Kheng got out of his hammock, stood up, stretched his back and observed the familiar surroundings. For Kheng this was the best part of the day, before the heat and humidity began to build, and before the rest of the town woke up and disturbed all of the dust that had spent a whole night trying to settle down.

Kheng untied the end of his hammock from the trunk of the old jackfruit tree at the rear of the bank's compound. With a swift pull on the thin rope it slipped away from its moorings, and he carefully rolled it up and put it in his bag. The way of tying-up his hammock was something he'd learned a long time ago in the army. If the enemy was nearby while you were camped out in the forest you could quickly pull away the hammock without fiddling with complicated knots, and then silently disappear into the undergrowth without being spotted. It was surprising that his old combat skill had become a useful life-skill that he could apply to his current career as the guard at the bank. Kheng had long since retired from the army. He'd been barely a man when he was signed up, but had stuck with the life and somehow survived more than thirty years of service. He finally left once he felt he was too old to keep going. He wasn't connected or educated to become an officer with a desk job, and wasn't quick enough to keep up with the younger blood. Besides, the war was long since over and there was a comfortable peace to the country. So, most of all, he hadn't felt he needed to serve any more. He would have long since retired from all work if it wasn't for his wife constantly nagging at him while he was at home. His having a job seemed to calm her down a bit, whilst simultaneously reducing the contact time available for her to be irritated by him.

For the last seven years, Kheng had quietly been performing the duty of the night guard at the Maklai provincial branch of the Khoyleng Bank. The bank didn't have a day guard. Old Papa Han had managed the branch for the last thirty years and had never seen the point in having one. Maklai was a respectable sleepy provincial town with respectable and sleepy people. They would never show such unpatriotic disrespect towards the establishment of their country as to denigrate one of their great financial institutions. For Papa Han, there was very little point in wasting money on a guard that wasn't needed. The bank was supposed to look after money, not squander it needlessly. Papa Han had only employed Kheng due to the pressure from the head office in the capital to show at least some tokenistic acknowledgement of their security policies.

Kheng would arrive for work every afternoon, just as the bank employees were locking up at 4.30pm. After a long night of guard duty, once Mr Tann, the head bank clerk, had returned to the bank and opened up the front doors at 8.00am each morning, he would head home. Kheng had been in the job for seven years now, and it was a lifestyle that suited him perfectly. Officially, his task was to patrol the compound around the bank throughout the night and then report any problems to the head clerk the next morning. For seven years Mr Tann observed that Kheng had arrived on time each evening, and left on time the following morning. As a result of this devoted service, every month Mr Tann handed over the slim envelope with Kheng's basic salary. They had both stuck fastidiously to this routine and Kheng was regarded as a highly reliable member of staff and an asset to the provincial branch. However, in Kheng's entire time at the bank, no one had ever actually checked up on him during the night to see if he was okay, or that he was even present. Kheng was by no means a slow-witted man, and had quickly picked up on this gap in the bank's HR management process.

When Kheng had first started in the job, each day he would bring his dinner with him in his old army rucksack. After a few months of the job, Kheng had got into the habit of packing his tattered standard issue hammock in the small rucksack as well. By 9.00pm, if not before, his part of the street was always very quiet, and he could set up his sleeping arrangements in the compound at the back of the bank. This way he could get in a good night's sleep and wake up with the rising sun and the crowing of the neighbouring cockerels. He would be packed up long before anyone started using the street again. The town's early risers would see the diligent guard dutifully guarding the premises, once they'd left their homes to vie for the freshest and best cuts of meat from the Maklai market.

By the end of his first year of employment, Kheng had

also concluded that the total lack of supervision over him meant that there was little point in bothering to bring his dinner with him either. When he had started in the job he had always brought with him a small series of metal pots that linked together. The first was filled with sticky rice, the next had some vegetables and the last a small piece of meat or a boiled egg. That way, as it got dark he would be able to sit and eat his meal before putting up his hammock. After a while he just brought the rucksack with the hammock. Once it was dark, around seven o'clock, he could simply slip out through the front gate, put the padlock back so it looked like the bank's entrance was still secure, and sneak home for his dinner. This would conveniently remove the drudgery of having to prepare something himself in the afternoon, put it in pots, bring it to work, eat his semi-cold food and then wash everything up with the outside tap. It was much easier to return and join the family at the time that his wife did the cooking. He had told his wife that the dinner break had all been agreed with the head clerk at the bank, and that Old Papa Han also approved. After all, the old man was a reasonable and respected gentleman who could see how unfair it was to make an employee work during a meal time when the regular daytime bank employees got a two-hour lunch break. After giving his food an hour or so to settle in his stomach Kheng would scuttle discreetly back to the bank, through the main gate, and relock the padlock. He'd been doing this for more than six years now, and no one had ever noticed. More importantly to Kheng, it had never mattered either. Old Papa Han had been right, Maklai was an uneventful and peaceful little town and the need for a guard was at best an extravagance. Of course, the occasional disreputable person stole the occasional disreputable chicken from the occasional yard, or sent their kids to pilfer the fruit from a neighbour's garden, but that was all part of normal life, it wasn't really seen as crime. No one would ever dare to dream of committing a real crime like a bank robbery. When fruit went missing from a well-tended custard-apple tree, people muttered under their breath a bit and whinged in closed circles about their miscreant neighbours. A bank robbery on the other hand had serious consequences. A person could be ostracised from their community, become an embarrassment to their family, or even go to jail. Worse still, the wife of such a ne'er-do-well of questionable morality might have to start going to a different market to avoid the shame of facing her regular cronies at the vegetable stalls. An even more terrible fate beyond that could involve your mother-in-law deciding to move your wife and family back in with her while you were behind bars and unable to prevent her from doing so. She might well help your wife to sell off your house and all your belongings whilst you were doing time and were powerless to do anything about it. Dealing with these matriarchs, particularly from the perspective of one whose unlawful activity had put the matriarch to the trouble of dismantling their son-in-law's life to maintain their social position, was not worth the aggravation for even the most hardened criminal. No, the likelihood of somebody committing grand-theft from a bank in the middle of the night was as improbable as a mother-in-law failing to bring up the subject of your limited salary each time she visited. It was a comfort to know that defending a provincial bank from armed robbers was the lowest-risk guarding job you could ever have in Maklai. It was undoubtedly for this reason that over the years Mr Tann had been quite astute in not bothering to waste his time checking up on Kheng.

Now that the sun was rising higher in the sky, the street

outside the entrance of the bank was bustling with life. The throng was mainly people going to the market, to either sell or buy. It was a daily activity that was at the heart of a life that didn't demand people to plan beyond the immediate. Tomorrow was too far off to think about today. The people with office jobs wouldn't be venturing out for another hour or so. As Kheng's shift was nearing its end he positioned himself beside the coconut palm that grew at the side of the pillar of the main gate. There was an old plastic chair that he used to sit on and observe the main street as the townsfolk woke from their slumber and gradually brought renewed life to the emptiness and quietness.

Just after seven o'clock the workmen that were assigned to the road works in the street outside the bank would be back to their labours and bring Kheng some added entertainment. Recently the town's streets had been getting a revamp, and new large concrete storm drains were being installed in deep trenches at the sides of all the roads and streets. For some reason this work had started at the beginning of the rainy season and the residents had suffered considerable disruption. The process involved digging up the old dirt roads, grading the roads, putting down soil, digging that back up, re-grading it again, digging up old drains, piling pre-cast concrete rings in the lanes, and then digging unconnected parts of huge deep trenches as the mood took them. The work-teams would then move their excavation circus to the next street along, with the intention to return and put everything back together at an undetermined date in the distant future.

Those residents next to these roads suffered the extremes of either flooding, as the earthworks prevented the flow of storm water away from their house, or finding that they now had a water-filled moat across their threshold where the trench excavation team had been better resourced than the drainage team, and got digging several months ahead.

However, the dry season was drawing near and the challenge of excess water was being replaced by the excessive dust that all the digging and grading produced. Over the last few weeks, work had started on the street in front of the bank. Some kid barely old enough to ride a moto had been enthusiastically running the huge backhoe that had gouged a deep trench along the side of the main street. The shop owners and residents had needed to go and buy planks of wood to construct makeshift gangways for the customers to balance their way across. Later a cement mixing truck had been used to pour the foundations in the trench, and yesterday a different machine had been used to drop in the large pre-cast concrete rings. A few workers had then started cementing up the gaps.

The construction activity was all fascinating stuff for Kheng, as it provided some much appreciated activity to an otherwise uneventful job. He was a practical man interested in practical things. Besides, usually nothing of note took place that could distract him from counting the time until the head clerk arrived to relieve Kheng from his guarding within the padlocked compound. Inevitably, monitoring the construction of the drainage works had become something of an addictive pastime. This morning, however, things were different.

5. The Dream

Kheng stared out of the gate and into the street. His thoughts were not with the development of the town's roads, as he would have liked them to be. Instead he was deliberating a vision that was engulfing his mind which he just couldn't shake. The previous night Kheng had drifted to sleep with pleasant thoughts about Papa Han's send-off. He had pondered with satisfaction the good turn out from the well-wishers, and how Papa Han would have been happy that so many friends had come to see him off and enjoy the spectacle. He had also thought about how he would use his own store of fireworks in the box under his house to a similar effect. Kheng had drifted off into a deep and content sleep. His gentle snoring through the darkness acted as a kindly grunt-like conversation for any passing bat or lizard that was looking for unobtrusive company. However, his usually peaceful slumber had been greatly disturbed and he had experienced a dream that had troubled him deeply. Normally he could never remember his dreams, and their imagery would dissipate into the air around him as he became more aware of being awake. However, this particular night time vision seemed to have stuck with him like an obstinate gecko on an insect-ridden ceiling. For much of the morning since he had woken, vivid and obscure images had swum through his head in a way he had never experienced before from a dream.

It seemed important to Kheng that he try to remember the dream so that he could understand it. Gradually he drew the disparate fragments from his memory and pieced together the odyssey that his dream had taken him on. At the start of the vision there had been a full and bright moon. It had risen up from behind a large tree. The moon had shone brightly. At first it felt like it must be the dry-season moon, tinged orange, large and glowing as the light battled through the heat and the dust to make its presence felt. However, the Kheng in the dream had not been fooled by this facade, this deceitful ambience of pretence. The Kheng that occupied the dream world knew very well that the moon that he was looking at was made from a liquid gold, hot and tempting, but too lethal and too far away for him to grab and claim for himself. He watched the false liquid moon, captivated as its form seemed to pulse, expand and rise but never really change. Some of the gold from the liquid hot globe dripped down from the sky. It landed on him even though the metal moon was near to the horizon and not above him. The gold splashed on his skin. Kheng instinctively flinched, he knew that the gold was white hot, but it didn't hurt, it just made him warm. Then from nowhere a large wild boar had appeared in front of the moon and faced Kheng with a gleam in its eye. It snorted a bit, and shook its head so that the tusks shone in the moonlight, brightly bathed in the golden glow and as sharp as bayonets. It cleared its throat and, following a grunt from its rumpled snout, the wild boar began to address Kheng in a very well-spoken but urgent voice: "The buffalo is a triangle. It's a triangle I'm telling you!"

The reiteration seemed to carry a rather frustrated tone. Frustration clearly aimed at Kheng. As quickly as it had appeared, the wild boar vanished from the sky. Almost immediately, Kheng's Aunt Kaylin had appeared from behind the moon with a scowl across her lined and cruel face. Waving her bamboo stick, she leaned forward, her face close to his like a bully trying to intimidate and instil fear. She ordered him to run to the market to buy her whisky, and there'd be trouble if he came home without any, and no mistake. It was at that point that Kheng had woken up in a cold sweat, and an angry Aunt Kaylin was where the vision had to end.

The dream had troubled Kheng greatly. As he never remembered dreams, to remember this rather disturbing series of events with such clarity was very concerning. His wife was a great believer in dreams. In the years before Kheng started his night shift job, which meant sleeping at the bank, his wife would often wake him in the middle of the night and talk him through the details of whatever visions had just visited her. That way she wouldn't forget them. Luckily she had never called on Kheng to remember the details the next day. In his half-awake state when receiving the narrative Kheng usually fell back to sleep none the wiser. The following day his wife would then review the dream in great detail with their neighbour, Mama Tae, who sold rattan furniture from underneath her stilt house that was next door to theirs. More often than not, if they concluded that the visions in the dream were particularly significant they would assign numbers to different parts of the imagery and then go and buy a lottery ticket to match the dream. Sometimes that worked and they'd get a bit of cash out of it. Often it didn't. When his wife and Mama Tae did produce some mild returns from the lottery, the dreamology was proven as irrefutable fact. When it failed to produce the cash then clearly they'd made a mistake in their interpretation. The failure to generate income was never the fault of the dream. Kheng rarely paid much attention to it all. The very fact that it kept his wife and Mama Tae entertained without disturbing him too much was sufficient reason to passively allow the study of dreams to be part of the household goings on.

Kheng continued to deliberate about his dream. He wondered whether his relaxed approach to dream interpretation was because he'd never really had a dream worth interpreting before. Now that he'd had one, he was almost intrigued enough to ask his wife about it. Obviously he couldn't mention it at work as it would be effectively admitting to sleeping on the job. He was wise enough by now to avoid that trap.

6. Manager

Across town at the Tamarind Hotel, Mr Hua Lin was finishing his breakfast. He was slowly pulling his noodles to his mouth with his chop sticks in a very deliberate fashion to avoid having any of the soupy liquid splatter down onto his new tie. He had brought both of his two new ties with him for his attendance at the formal lunch later that day. On the way down to Maklai he had been racked with indecision. A bad first impression would put him on the back foot, and the right tie for the right impression was all important. Fortunately, he had woken with more certainty and clarity than when he'd draped both of his ties over the back of the chair and studied them intently before he'd gone to bed. He had reached purposefully for the blue one immediately after brushing his teeth and donning a salmon pink shirt. He then put on his jacket and checked himself out in the small bathroom mirror. The deep and formal blue of the traditional silk said he meant business. It showed he was a fair man and an approachable person, one who was respectful of tradition and aware of his cultural heritage. However, it also seemed to convey his need for polite dialogue and sensible behaviour. Hua Lin was aware that he was asking quite a lot from his tie. However, it would be his first time to meet the staff from

Maklai branch of the bank, as well as some of their more important clients, and first impressions were everything.

Having addressed the tie dilemma, Hua Lin was able to turn his thoughts to the broader issues that surrounded his move to Maklai. He'd never been to the province before, or even travelled such a distance from the capital where he was brought up. Until now he'd never really had any interest to venture so precariously from his comfort zone. Why would you want to drift out to the provinces when you already lived in the capital? Such a move was very much swimming against the tide. As a privileged capital dweller he already had the thing that those trapped in the provinces enviously craved. However, Mr Hua Lin was young and ambitious, and he was finding that opportunities to climb the ladder at the main bank in the Khoyleng head office were few and far between. Competition between his colleagues for the good jobs at the bank was always high. His family was not strongly connected in a world where cronyism dominated as the governing philosophy. Although he played to his charm and intelligence, so that he was liked and respected in his office, the superficial details would only get him so far. Without family connections he was unlikely to move beyond the level of clerk for at least another fifteen years. Meanwhile, offering to forgo the privileges of life in the capital, and venture as a fearless pioneer into the untamed provinces to represent the bank's interests, meant that he was immediately considered for the management position. In general, the directors of the bank in the capital were very wary of any provincial staff that had been recruited locally. They lacked the drive and the superior education that Khoyleng people possessed. They were simply not in the same class, or able to think progressively in the same way. At best you could consider them as antiquated, but often archaic was a more appropriate label. From the perspective of the management at the main Khoyleng Bank, it was far better to have one of their own overseeing the provinces to make sure the system didn't deviate from the requisite protocols and drift away from the bank's modern thinking. Mr Hua Lin had put his name forward to his supervisors as someone who would be prepared to take his education and experience out to the provinces for the greater good of the institution. His supervisors had been impressed.

Mr Hua Lin was not entirely sure he'd made the right decision about Maklai, now that he'd arrived. Maklai seemed very backward and old fashioned compared with Khoyleng. The Tamarind Hotel had been recommended as the best option for such a high-ranking visitor, but the furniture in the room was cheap and shabby. The aircon was the old-fashioned noisy type that disturbed his sleep. From what he'd seen of the town itself the previous day, it was very dusty and difficult to navigate. Large, incomplete drainage ditches seemed to cut across vital thoroughfares with little indication of alternative routes. For some reason almost every street had parts of deep trenches on either side with varying piles of dirt both in and at the side of the road, none of which appeared to provide any utility. There didn't seem to be much evidence of pipes getting put in, or how they would ever connect to each other. Hua Lin couldn't work out why they would do all the digging first and fail to put pipes in at the same time. If this was indicative of how people thought and worked in Maklai then he was going to have his work cut out managing the bank. There also seemed to be a lack of good clothes shops in Maklai. This absence of retailers was strongly reflected in what the local people were wearing, as they seemed to fail to keep up with or indeed care about modern trends.

The staff at the hotel were uniformed in locally made suits and skirts which seemed very backward in their design compared with what people were wearing in Khoyleng these days. Admittedly he'd only arrived the previous afternoon; however, during his first evening and his brief overview of the town, albeit with limited access, he had failed to spot any new-looking bars, expensive restaurants, or indeed very much to do at all. He assumed that to retain his sanity, after a while he'd probably have to start taking a night bus each Friday afternoon and go back to the city for the weekends.

Hua Lin looked up from his diminishing bowl of breakfast noodles and observed that his supervisor from the Khoyleng central bank was coming over to join him. His boss was also appropriately suited up and notably was sporting a demure crimson tie with a diagonal pattern. Hua Lin allowed himself an inward smile. He noted that his own choice of tie did not clash with that of his boss, and, more importantly, that his boss's tie would not achieve the same degree of first-impression impact that his blue one would. The day was already going well.

7. Opening

"Good morning, Mr Tann."

The head clerk, Mr Tann, had arrived with his usual delayed precision and air of apathy at about ten past eight. He paused for a moment while he acknowledged Kheng's presence on the other side of the large double gates. Kheng undid the padlock and swung the creaky gate inwards in order to let his supervisor through.

"Nice day today, Mr Tann. Not too cold this morning."

Kheng, who was in an unusually alert mood as a result of his dream, had decided to keep the conversation ticking along in the absence of a response from his supervisor. His enthusiasm for interacting with a fellow staff member was also driven by his excitement for the staff outing that was planned for later that day.

Mr Tann reached into his tattered leather satchel and produced the excessively fat bunch of keys that represented the non-personnel element of bank security. He rifled through the bunch to try and locate the one amongst the many that would release the bank from its current impenetrable state. While he did so he considered Kheng's initial observation, and eventually replied.

"Yes. I suppose it might be. A nice day."

Mr Tann decided to reference his comment, as it had

been a while since Kheng's second attempt at communication. His reply was thoughtful and yet a little distracted. He had never managed to accept that greetings were courteous, albeit benign, remarks. Instead of respectfully offering a benign response back to complete the formality he gave any observation directed at him his serious deliberation, and returned with a considered opinion. Today's almost positive response from Mr Tann was quite uplifting compared with most days. It was unusual to get anything from him that wasn't laced with a gloomy undertone. Seemingly, today wasn't most days.

Mr Tann continued to sift erratically through his heavy bunch of keys until he found the one he was looking for. Having applied it to the key hole and jiggled it around until it connected properly with the ancient workings, the key finally turned and the equally geriatric front door swung open, shuddering and creaking painfully as it did so.

"Not as cold as last month in the early mornings. Still it could all change again," persisted Kheng.

"Indeed. Remind me to ask the administrator to organise oil for those hinges, Kheng."

Kheng nodded and smiled at Mr Tann in an agreeable fashion.

"It was a nice send-off yesterday for Old Papa Han, wasn't it, Mr Tann? Good fireworks. Some of those rockets cleared the road at the bottom of the hill. And the firecrackers were really loud. I imagine Old Papa Han would have been very pleased to see that all those people turned out to send him on his way."

Kheng continued in the absence of a response from the head clerk:

"I'll make my way home then, Mr Tann. I might try and get in a bit of sleep before the staff lunch with the visitors that have come down from head office."

Mr Tann shrugged. There had never been a staff luncheon for the bank employees before today, and he was rather unnerved by the general concept. He was particularly hesitant about the whole idea as the social event would involve key clients attending as well. It was what the man from head office had told him to organise, and so he had done it. Neither he nor his staff had received suitable training for that eventuality. They knew how to fill in the bank's paperwork and record the transfer of money. Representing the bank's interests at social occasions and exuding personality to entertain important customers had never been a skill they were expected to show. Worse still, a couple of men from Khoyleng's management were expected to attend. It wasn't something that he was particularly looking forward to. He wasn't quite sure why everyone from the bank had to go, including Kheng. Of course Kheng was a good and loyal employee and well respected in his position as guard. However, at lunches with important people from a different layer of society, of education and wealth, then it was important to say the right thing, and that should necessitate the exclusion of those who only knew how to use common language and not the more formal and correct grammar. There was a high risk of embarrassment.

Kheng considered that his routine engagement of Mr Tann in light conversation was completed. He carefully stepped along the slightly bendy wooden planks that had been laid over the drainage trench and uncovered pipe in front of the bank, and headed across the street. He valued his interactions with Mr Tann, and felt that today's jovial banter had gone particularly well. This was partly because he rarely got to speak to anyone until the head clerk came and opened up the bank, but also because it was good practice to be on jovial terms with your employer. It would be morally and emotionally far more difficult for his employer to sack him later on if something did go wrong. For example, if his absence from guard duty around dinnertime each night should come to Mr Tann's attention, there would be an obligation to let it slide if he promised to improve, rather than bring down the punishment set out in the bank's code of conduct.

***

Lunchtime arrived and Mr Tann dutifully herded his staff from behind their desks so that they all made their way to the Sou-Rehn Restaurant on the other side of town. The entire bank staff, twelve in all, including the part-time cleaner and Kheng, had been invited. The bank would of course have to be left unguarded in order for all of the staff to join in; however, this reduction in security was normally the case at lunchtimes anyway. The employees had tried to be cheerful and upbeat about their excursion. They had never been on a work outing before. However, it was difficult to get too celebratory knowing they would have to get back to work at one thirty and be sufficiently sober to avoid giving away too much of the bank's money by accident. They had hoped for an evening meal at the restaurant. However, the suit from head office insisted on a lunchtime event so that he would be able to leave immediately afterward and be driven back to his home in Khoyleng by evening. With a number of Maklai's more important businessmen attending the meal, the staff would need to be on their best behaviour. Failure to do so would mean several weeks of suffering the silent but targeted broodings of Mr Tann as he skulked around the bank. This was definitely not a social occasion, it was work.

The table for the meal had been set out in the back room of the restaurant before the bank staff had arrived. Several long tables had been joined together, each one adorned with a cheap off-white table cloth. On each of the tables were various small dishes. Their contents of pork ribs, fried vegetables, cabbage, and diced chicken with ginger were covered in cling-film to keep the flies off until the guests were ready to eat. Once seated, and whilst the formalities were being completed, rice and soup would be brought out and served to the people in the order that the waitresses perceived rank or importance.

Shortly after twelve o'clock, the two gentlemen from head office arrived in their car at the front of the restaurant. Mr Tann had been respectfully hovering in a shady area by the entrance so he would be able to step out and greet them formally. He shook the hand of the elder gentleman first, assuming him to be the superior member of the party, and then outstretched an equally awkward and limp hand for Mr Hua Lin to shake.

Mr Tann carefully ushered his honoured guests towards the back room of the Sou-Rehn restaurant and ensured they were seated in the middle of the top table. He then sat himself and his wife alongside them so everyone could see that he was not too far below on the scale of importance. Other local businessmen and honoured guests were ushered in alongside, and then the regular bank staff took up the remaining seats at the periphery. Mr Tann didn't look like a man who was comfortable with his role of acting figurehead and socialite. In his more regular working role he mainly sat in his office overseeing the bookkeeping and ledgers. It wasn't a very busy bank so there was not much to oversee and not too many mistakes were ever found. Both Mr Tann and the clerks that he supervised knew that it was the clerks who did the actual work. The expansion of Mr Tann's terms of reference to flamboyant host in the absence of Old Papa Han was not the most welcome of additions. However, as the chain of command had diminished above him, Mr Tann was willing to accept that to fill the position of bank manager meant that his increasing status brought with it a little more responsibility. His wife had a similarly conflicting expression. On the one hand, her sour countenance indicated that she didn't particularly want to be part of this level of social responsibility. There was also an air of superiority of one who had waited a long time for her status to finally be raised to the extent that she felt socially entitled. This elevated demeanour was not lost on the provincial bank's non-managerial staff, who were mainly bunched together at the other end of the tables following a 'safety in numbers' approach to social survival.

Kheng wasn't completely in the loop as to why the bank was having a lunchtime gathering. Just that one was happening, and that he was expected to go. He had assumed it must be as a mark of respect to the passing of their long-serving provincial manager, Papa Han. He mingled with the other bank staff and took his place next to the cleaner at the far end of the tables. It was a good place to observe the event without having to contribute too much. He noted with a degree of satisfaction that a senior manager from Khoyleng and his equally dapper and suited colleague had travelled to Maklai to join the auspicious event and show their support. It was only right that after all of Papa Han's dedication to the bank and to the town in general that head office should make the effort to show their respect.

Once the soup and rice had been delivered to the table, the official in the red striped tie stood up with a purposeful air. He did up the middle of his three suit buttons to bring attention to the fact he was wearing an expensive suit, which greatly emphasised his importance, and gave the audience a chance to drink in the magnitude of his presence. He then proceeded to deliver a lengthy speech. From one perspective, the lengthy period of rambling that he managed to deliver was quite admirable considering that he had never known Papa Han or, before yesterday evening, had even been to Maklai province before. However, on the other hand it did mean that the soup went cold. On balance he didn't particularly ingratiate himself to the Maklai bank staff who were on their first ever works outing and politely abstaining from their meal while they waited for him to finish. After his verbose deliberations the boss from Khoyleng finally introduced his suited colleague in the blue tie.

"Before we eat, I would like to acquaint you with my colleague Mr Hua Lin. He will be replacing Mr Han as your new Provincial Branch Manager."

He turned to Hua Lin and gestured that he should also stand.

"Perhaps you would like to say some words before we start."

Mr Tann coughed a little as if he was choking to a degree, which would be rather unlikely as they had not been able to eat anything yet. The cling-film on the side plates was still clinging, and the soup was firmly congealing in the ever-cooling bowls, waiting for the end of the formalities. His wife somehow managed to wring her facial expression into one that was ever so slightly more sour than before. Kheng observed this achievement with a sense of awe for the seemingly impossible and a feeling of deep sympathy for Mr Tann. The new appointment of a Provincial Branch Manager was breaking news to everyone from the Maklai branch. The previous lack of news was not wholly unexpected, as reports within the bank only tended to gravitate upwards towards the management in Khoyleng, and rarely downwards. Even then, most reports got stuck, or lost on the desk of an intermediate level of management during the journey. Many a managerial meeting had been opened and closed with comments about never receiving any reports. It was therefore not at all surprising that reports never worked their way back down the chain to the Maklai staff. However, this lack of communication usually meant that people made assumptions from which they extracted their own news. In this case, everyone had assumed Mr Tann was the natural successor to the manager position. They had also assumed that the lunch was orchestrated, at least in part, to enable the bosses from Khoyleng to share this predictable outcome with the staff and distinguished clients.

Mr Hua Lin dutifully stood as commanded. He also buttoned his jacket, to create a pause in which the gravitas could build, as if it were all part of the Khoyleng management training. In truth, he'd hoped to avoid a pre-lunch speech. The bank staff and honoured business guests were already looking with glum expressions at their deteriorating soup. As last speaker, he would be the one they remembered as they finally got the chance to drain some of the insipidly cold broth. He was also the one left with very little to say, as his boss had already covered most of what was possible in the event of knowing nothing about where you were or who you were talking to. Hua Lin cleared his throat and began:

"I would just like to say that I am delighted to meet all of you, and look forward to working with you all. It's always a bit daunting when a new boss arrives but I'm sure there will be very few changes to start with. The Khoyleng Bank has always had very clear rules and regulations so we will continue to follow them and provide our excellent service to the people of Maklai."

With that Mr Hua Lin unbuttoned his suit jacket and returned to his chair, hoping that in light of his brevity the staff would barely notice the speech's impact on the temperature of the soup.

And thus, the staff of the Maklai provincial branch learned that the man who had been standing before them, Mr Hua Lin, was to become the new provincial branch manager. Polite smiles and nods of appreciation emanated from the gathering. Some started to peel cling-film from much needed sustenance whilst others politely ladled lukewarm soup into the small bowls of neighbouring diners. However, the renewed activity failed to cover up a number of hushed mutterings and raised eyebrows of surprise. It had always been assumed by the staff that Mr Tann, the head clerk, would automatically fill Papa Han's slightly dusty and worn out shoes. No one had realised that a recruitment process had taken place that had failed to include Mr Tann as a candidate, or indeed made itself known to the provincial bank. There was an unspoken understanding or shared telepathy in Maklai that had long since established Mr Tann's place in the bank's lineage. Such long-standing devotion to the institution meant that his right to the manager's job was an inevitability. Therefore, no one had thought to consult Khoyleng head office about this, assuming they were in on the unspoken assumption as well.

Mr Tann was not pleased, and he eyed Mr Hua Lin suspiciously. To Mr Tann, this Hua Lin looked like the sort of 'new ideas' person who would turn up and start changing things, bringing in new initiatives where the old ones had served them just fine. He'd already changed Mr Tann's expectations about a future, where he'd been anticipating the opportunity to skulk in Papa Han's old office and generally avoid having to meet many customers until he could eventually retire.

Kheng eyed Mr Hua Lin with complete indifference. The only impact this new manager would ever have on his life was in that exact moment, on account of the soup's deterioration from piping hot to not warm enough. However, it was still free soup – so Kheng was ahead either way.

8. Ms Win-Kham

After the meal the workforce started to filter out to the front of the restaurant and shuffled around for a while trying to be sociable but without falling into the trench for the storm-water pipes that had cut them off from the road. Overall they were hoping someone amongst the lucky few from the bank who had their own cars would organise them and take them back to work. It was during this period of non-committal milling that Ms Win-Kham took the opportunity to introduce herself to Mr Hua Lin. She began her approach with a very reverential but subtle bow, and then proceeded to give the suited gentlemen highlights of her résumé.

"It is so wonderful that someone of your skills and experience has come to help us in the province, Mr Hua Lin. I am Ms Win-Kham. I've been working at the bank five years now. Before that I worked in accounting at the telephone company. I was there for only three years and then I got my chance at the bank. It's a wonderful place to work, and such friendly people. I'm sure you're going settle in very quickly. We will benefit so much from someone like you who has been working at the head office in the capital and has such great experience and knowledge to share with us. I know we will learn a lot."

Hua Lin smiled back politely, and with slight embarrassment. He wasn't used to getting such a barrage of compliments, but he enjoyed the shameless ingratiation from the woman all the same. Most of the other staff seemed to be deliberately avoiding making any eye contact with him for fear they would be expected to interact with the new manager. This one seemed to be a bit more on the ball than some of the others. He estimated she was late twenties to early thirties, attractive but appropriately and conservatively dressed for an employee at a bank. Her traditional skirt was clearly an expensive one, normally the type reserved for attending a wedding or similar grand event, showing that she'd made every effort to impress. Other staff, he'd noted, had come straight from the bank, in what would be their usual working attire.

Hua Lin decided to reply with a few non-committals of his own:

"I'm sure I am going to feel very happy here. Everyone today has been extremely kind and welcoming. I really hope I can bring things forward, and more in line with the bank's current thinking."

Ms Win-Kham smiled coyly at him and started playing with her hair, which draped over her shoulder.

"I do so look forward to working with you. You're just what this bank needs."

Hua Lin made a slightly nervous cough. He straightened his blue tie a little and re-buttoned his jacket. He felt uneasy around overly confident women, particularly if they were attractive women, with reasonable jobs and a similar level of intellect. There was something disconcerting about them. You couldn't quite talk to them like they were other men, but you couldn't treat them like they were just beer girls either. From Hua Lin's perspective, these types of women moved within a tricky and poorly understood stratum of the social ladder. There was a middle ground somewhere between the extremes that was difficult to deal with. Hua Lin had never quite worked out where this middle ground was, and as a result was very mistrustful of the whole thing. Ms Win-Kham took the awkward pause after his reply as an opportunity to engage him further.

"It's so nice to hear that you will be making sure all the rules and regulations of the bank are followed. It'll be just like they do at the head bank in the capital. I'm sure our customers will be very impressed. I look forward to your guidance and support. The Khoyleng Bank has such very good systems and dedication to the rules is so important in a bank. If there is any help you need from me as you are settling in, please, you only have to ask. I really want to learn more from you so that we can make the provincial branch more efficient."

"Well that's very kind, Ms Win-Kham. Please, you must excuse me now. I should talk to Mr Sabkee from head office before he starts to travel back to Khoyleng."

Having made a plausible excuse, followed by a gesture to indicate that he needed to remove himself before an embarrassing silence injected itself to the brewing lull in conversation, Mr Hua Lin strode purposefully towards the group of men that were still lingering just outside the building and smoking cigarettes. As he approached the group his supervisor called him over and offered him a smoke. He immediately felt much more at ease. Silences were rarely embarrassing when you were in a group of men. It was well understood that if no one had anything to say then simply not saying something and then shuffling your feet a bit was an equally effective and comfortable way to communicate with each other.

Ms Win-Kham teetered across an array of wobbly planks that connected the restaurant to the road, and then wandered over to where Mr Tann had parked his aging mini-van under the shade of a large tree. Being first in the transport queue would mean that when the others were ready to leave she could grab the front seat and not have to squash into the tiny half-seats at the back of the vehicle and crease up her best skirt. As she waited, her gaze returned to the restaurant. Mr Hua Lin was politely seeing off his boss from the roadside. The man with the red tie had entered the back seat of his large black town car and was giving Hua Lin some last minute advice before ordering his driver to start the journey back to the capital. She was impressed by what she had seen of her new boss. Mr Hua Lin was clearly a man who valued how he presented himself. He also understood when brevity of speech was a priority. He was polite and well spoken. He was clearly nervous around women, at least around some women. He was nervous around her anyway, and that might be just what was needed. She decided that Hua Lin was a man who meant business and dealt with things efficiently. This was all relative of course. In a sleepy town like Maklai lethargy was a quality to be aspired to, so as not to disturb the quiet rhythm of non-confrontational monotony. He was also young and was using his over-confidence to cover his lack of experience. In the right hands he could be malleable and influenced. In this regard, he was probably not someone who was going to stay still for too long. He wouldn't want to be treading water in the murky pond of Maklai whilst other ambitious people paddled their way up-stream to splash about in the crystal clear waterfalls of their careers in Khoyleng. Most importantly he was potentially someone that would favour marrying a woman who knew how to support his career. He would choose such a woman to further his success rather than marry for love, even if that meant spending every day living in constant fear of his wife.

Win-Kham watched as Hua Lin closed the car door of his supervisor and stood back as the car pulled away and began its journey out of town and onwards to the big city. Hua Lin continued to watch from the roadside as the car reached the end of the street and turned left on the road toward Khoyleng. There was something about him reminiscent of a small child being abandoned outside the school gates on the first day of term.

There was a certain amount of vulnerability hiding behind that blue tie. Ms Win-Kham smiled. The door clicked behind her and she realised that Mr Tann had finally made it over to open his car, ushering her away from the front passenger seat so that his fuming wife might be slightly appeased by not having to sit in the back. Ms Win-Kham didn't mind having to climb into the seat behind and squash in with the others. After all, the opportunity she had been hoping for had finally come along. Her days of having to sit in the back with the other, lower and unimportant, people were numbered.

9. Vision Interpretation

Kheng had walked home after the lunch with his colleagues from the bank. It wasn't too far, about half an hour if he took a leisurely pace. He hadn't wanted to ask the others for a lift as they were mostly going straight back to the bank for the afternoon's work. On reaching his home he allowed himself to doze for an hour or so on the bamboo framed bed-like bench under the shade of his stilted house. A small siesta would allow the remaining effects of too much cold fish soup to wear off. It was during this dozing that Kheng decided he should broach the subject of the troubling dream to his wife, Nelea. He knew by doing this he was being his own worst enemy. Inevitably she would get all enthusiastic and over the top about the possible hidden messages embedded in the events. This was the last thing Kheng wanted. On the other hand, he was desperate to share his dream experience with somebody and try to figure out why he was suddenly remembering this haunting imagery with such clarity.

When Nelea returned from the market, Kheng told her that the previous night he'd had an interesting dream. Before he could get any further, Nelea insisted on fetching Mama Tae from next door to listen to Kheng's description.

Before standing near the small bush that demarked their close boundary and calling loudly for her neighbour, Nelea explained to Kheng that she was a bit handy at identifying the numerology aspect of dreams and it usually led to her buying a lottery ticket. However, Mama Tae was the one who had many more years' experience in understanding the true underlying meanings. Kheng was aware that this was the group dynamic. It had been made clear many times before. However, he had really just wanted to share his burden a little with his wife, rather than seek to benefit from the full service for dreamology that was locally available.

Kheng pulled an 'I should have seen this coming' expression and complained that he wasn't sure he wanted Mama Tae involved. He pointed out that she could be a bit over the top when doing this sort of thing and it always seemed to involve praying to tree spirits. He'd rather keep it within the family for now. Neighbours and tree spirits were a secondary priority. However, so far as Nelea was concerned, Kheng's argument held very little weight. Between the three of them, Mama Tae was by far the most likely to come up with a plausible explanation for a dream that needed one. Also, Nelea could already hear Mama Tae calling back to her from the back of her house. She was saying that she was on her way once she'd finished plucking the chicken her sister-in-law had given her earlier that morning in exchange for a rattan rice basket.

Having been duly alerted to an exciting opportunity of impromptu dream interpretation, Mama Tae appeared from the side of the building, a few small feathers caught in wisps of her long and slightly unkempt hair, confirming the reason for her slight delay.

"Well, we can't do this out here! The spirits don't like to

let their secrets be shared under the bright glare of the afternoon sun. We must go inside."

Mama Tae ushered her neighbours into their home and then climbed up the short ladder into the house behind them, a bright gleam shining in her aging and wizened eyes.

Kheng sat down near to the cooking fire to the rear of the large wooden room. He'd been a distant observer of dream interpretation before and so was resigned to the fact that it would have to take place in the darkest, smokiest corner. Nelea sat near him. Mama Tae lowered herself inelegantly on the opposite side of the fire place.

"So, I hear you've been dreaming, Mr Kheng."

Her voice had a wise and knowing tone, with a slight gruffness that had developed from years of drawing thick smoke from bamboo pipes and listening contentedly to the water gurgling in the pipe's base as she did so. It was as if she'd understood long ago that this dream would be the pinnacle of Kheng's being, and that fate had moved him in next door especially so she would be on hand to interpret it. This was completely contrary to Kheng's assessment of the situation, and his years of neighbourly experience of Mama Tae told him there was nothing wise or knowing about her at all.

"Let us see if we can work out what journey this vision will take you on."

Mama Tae's gravelly tones became, at least superficially, even more wise and knowing. Nelea seemed delighted that Mama Tae was so into it. It was very rare that Nelea had something so special to contribute to their regular gossiping and deliberations on the spiritual. Normally, she was only able to talk about what she'd seen at the market that day and any gossip she'd heard about others. She never had any real good first-hand juicy information.

Meanwhile Mama Tae always had stories about the strange goings in on her village from when she was a child, the mystical implications of what had come to pass, and how the tree spirits would play their tricks and needed to be appeased.

"It is wise that you have chosen to sit around the fire, Mr Kheng. Before we can understand about the visions from your sleep, first we have to call upon the tree spirits to help us on our journey."

Mama Tae had specifically positioned herself by the cooking pots and where the cooking utensils were stored. She began poking with a large knife at the embers that remained from where Nelea had prepared lunch earlier in the day. Her efforts filled the room with a cloud of thick grey smoke and ash that was captured and swirled in the shafts of light that penetrated the gaps in the wooden planks of the walls.

Kheng reluctantly manoeuvred himself closer to the fire and sat opposite her. Nelea gathered herself in closer as well, but with rather more enthusiasm.

"Now!"

Mama Tae's yell almost made Kheng jump out of his skin. As she called out and dramatically waved her arms at the fire, her aged and bony fingers spread out as much as her arthritis would allow. There was an obscure sense of an eccentric pterodactyl about her. The flames of the fire flicked to life from the gust of air generated by Mama Tae's flapping about, and Kheng's legs became covered in a thin layer of ash. The old lady leaned forward muttering incantations, no doubt checking that the relevant spirits were on hand, before they delved into the essence of the reading. She stared Kheng in the eyes with fiery intensity, and dramatically whispered through her broken teeth:

"Now, Mr Kheng. Speak to me of your dream."

She sounded like she was trying to channel the voice of a spirit from beyond the grave. It was all a bit theatrical for Kheng's taste. Nelea grinned like a small child who was riding a bike without falling off for the first time. This was the most exciting thing to have happened in ages. Kheng was a little more wary of the whole thing. He'd also grown up in a village where tree spirits were part of the cultural fabric. He knew very well about the mischief and trouble they could bring, as well as the mischief others made on their behalf. He was a little unsure that he really needed to get them involved at this stage. However, seeing how much Nelea was enjoying herself, he felt compelled to explain his dream to the entire gathering, both human and spiritual.

Mama Tae seemed to be in a sort of possessed trance for much of Kheng's story. When he'd finished she looked down at the fire, muttered some more incantations and then stood up and kicked ash from the edge of the cooking area at the flames until they reduced again to smouldering embers. Once the dust had cleared and Kheng had stopped coughing, he could see Mama Tae walking across the room, silhouetted by the smoky light shining through the open door.

"I'm just going next door to get my pipe. I'll be back in a minute."

Kheng and Nelea decided some fresh air would be the way to go as well, and so followed her through the door and descended down the small ladder at the front of their wooden stilt home. They sat on the wide bamboo framed bed beneath the house waiting for Mama Tae to return. Eventually she emerged, pushing her way through the thin shrubbery that formed the nominal boundary between their properties, making bubbling noises with her long bamboo pipe as she did so. Mama Tae's mannerisms suggested that she was back to her normal non-possessed self. This was the version of the old lady that was always around at their house and gossiping incessantly with Nelea, much to Kheng's annoyance. She sat down next to Kheng and gurgled on her pipe a bit more. Kheng was trying to decide if the smoking was helping her deliberate further about the meaning of his vision, or if, in line with her higher status as dream interpreter, she was simply waiting to be consulted. Before long she looked up from her pipe with a thoughtful expression.

"Well, that was certainly an interesting dream. Clearly the tree spirits have gathered around you and are trying to tell you something important, Mr Kheng."

Kheng had already seen this coming. He'd passively experienced a number of dream interpretation conversations between the two women. It was a small house, his wife was a naturally loud speaker and Mama Tae's hearing was not what it had been, making most conversations at their place difficult to avoid. Interpretations could vary wildly, but there was one thing you could rely on without fail. Whatever the dream was about, at the centre of the whole thing there was always going to be a mischievous tree spirit causing as much trouble as possible.

"So what is your interpretation then, Mama Tae?"

Kheng was a practical man. He just needed to get to the key facts and then he could move on. There was no need to drag this out into a lengthy discussion.

"Your husband has never been one for patience has he, Nelea."

Mama Tae cackled a gravelly smoky cackle. She was always more cackly after a tree spirit encounter. It seemed to bring out the amateur dramatics side in her.

10. Meaning

Mama Tae took one last bubbly drag on her bamboo pipe before starting her analysis:

"We'll begin with the golden moon, Mr Kheng, as that was the first image in your dream. The moon could symbolise that something is becoming stronger in your life, or more dramatic. Meanwhile, gold can be about seeing new possibilities or opportunities. Of course gold is always about wealth as well."

Nelea was delighted with this, and let out a small 'whoop'.

"I knew it! Something becoming *stronger*, Kheng! Strength is always associated with the number four, and everyone knows that wealth is represented by the number eight. Four and eight. We've got our first two lottery numbers!"

Nelea could barely contain her excitement. Mama Tae waited for her to calm down a bit and stop shuffling around so much before continuing. It was really distracting from the delivery of mystic and intrigue that she was trying to capture.

"So, the starting point is strength, drama and opportunity. Let's move now to the next phase of the dream."

Kheng raised an eyebrow. He'd not re-told his dream as a series of phases, and so was surprised that 'phasing' was now becoming part of the interpretation process.

"The wild boar can represent behaviour that is intentionally disagreeable. It spoke to you of a buffalo and a triangle. Buffaloes tend to represent procrastination, and triangles are about creation."

Nelea saw an opportunity to leap in:

"Number three. Triangles. Three sides, three corners. The cycle of life has three phases: birth or rebirth, life and death. However you look at it, triangles in a dream give you the number three."

Mama Tae shot another withering look at Nelea, which seemed to capture a sense of frustration combined with the indulgence that a wise and learned master might condescendingly direct toward an eager but disruptive student.

Nelea was looking smug again. The hopes of a big win in the lottery were really picking up and with her big toe she started scratching the numbers into the soil below where she was sitting.

"Now, Mr Kheng, let's talk aunts. Aunts can be tricky at the best of times, even more so when it comes to dreaming about them. On the one hand they can bring a heightened sense of luck, or they can mean that your instincts about something are unusually accurate. On the other hand the presence of an aunt might mean that you are unlucky or perhaps that your gut feeling about something is wrong. They can be very contradictory things, aunts. And let's not forget she asked you to get whisky. The whisky in the dream suggests that you may go too far with an idea or things could get out of hand. However, combine this notion with the link to the aunt, and then taking something too far could be lucky for you. Or just plain wrong.

Depending on why the aunt is there, which is hard to tell."

Mama Tae put down the pipe on the bench behind her and put her hands in her lap.

"So there you are, Mr Kheng. That was my interpretation of your dream."

Kheng thought about it for a while before answering.

"So what we are saying is that something strong and dramatic related to wealth is coming up in my life involving disagreeable behaviour, procrastination and/or the cycle of life. This may be either lucky or unlucky, depending on whether my gut feelings are right or wrong, and then it will all go too far and get out of hand."

Mama Tae nodded sagely.

"Well what on earth does that mean then?"

Mama Tae paused for a moment and then breathed a deep and knowing sigh.

"I am merely the vessel by which the spirits have allowed you to elaborate on your vision. How you use this new knowledge that you have been blessed with is very much part of your own destiny."

Kheng frowned a long and hard frown. There was a good reason why he never told his dreams to Mama Tae from next door and he was annoyed for allowing himself to be tempted to change this well established routine.

Nelea could see that Kheng was about to get frustrated with Mama Tae and so decided to intervene.

"What it all means is that we need to buy a lottery ticket with the numbers four, eight and three. We also need a fourth number or it won't work as well. Are you 'in', Mama Tae? What number do we get for Kheng's Aunt Kaylin?"

Mama Tae collected her pipe from the bench and stood up.

"Off course I'm in, Nelea. Why wouldn't I be? We've

not had a good set of numbers like this for weeks. Aunts are very difficult when it comes to assigning numbers. Whisky can be a bit tricky as well. However, don't forget the pig or boar or whatever that animal was that was going on about the buffalo in the triangle. A pig can be either a seven, forty-seven or eighty-seven. However, we've already got the four and eight so I think we'll just add the seven. So then that's four and eight, and three and seven. I'm probably good for about ten tickets. We'll have to stop at the house first though so I can get some money."

With their satisfactory four-figure conclusion the two ladies stood up to get started on their mission.

"Grab an umbrella for me while I'm at the house as well, Nelea. I lost mine a few weeks back. It's a hot day and we'll need some shade while we walk down to the market and buy the tickets."

Before long the two ladies strode off in the direction of town under the shade of their colourful umbrellas and Kheng was left beneath his house to ponder over the riddle that Mama Tae had given him. Common sense told him that a dream as complicated as his didn't hold any spiritual weight. It was just a series of images to enable his mad neighbour to conjure up four numbers and whisk away his wife for the afternoon to waste all their money on lottery tickets. That's what common sense should have told him. Meanwhile, instinctively Kheng knew there was far more to his vision than that.

11. Security

"Afternoon, Mr Tann. Good day at work?"

It had been a week since the staff lunch at the Sou-Rehn Restaurant. The already uninspiring face of Mr Tann had fallen considerably in recent days. Kheng assumed it was a result of Mr Tann's learning that he was to become the servant of some youthful and green city dweller rather than take over the reins of the old master himself. The slumped demeanour that had alighted on Mr Tann after the staff outing still hadn't risen back up. Kheng wondered if it ever would. Mr Tann seemed to have the sort of face that would only ever deteriorate. It was unlikely to alternate regularly between a grey haggardness and a youthful glow depending on the mood at the time. However, Mr Tann's despondency wasn't going to deter Kheng from his routine of afternoon pleasantries. As was the case with the well-established morning attempts at verbal interaction, Kheng would always engage Mr Tann in a little light banter as the man made his way out of the bank as well. The event coincided with Kheng's arrival as night guard and had almost become part of his job over the years.

In order for Kheng to save up his variations on the morning weather conversation, in the afternoon he would normally ask about the day's goings-on at the bank, pry for a bit of gossip or as a last resort enquire about an update of the fiscal state of the country. In return Mr Tann would usually offer up a brief snippet of irrelevant financial information or have a whinge about someone who had annoyed him. He would then offer an appeasing conclusion, like 'oh well, another day under our belts then…' and shuffle out of the gate and head listlessly home. Seven years' worth of brief semi-insightful snippets had given Kheng a surprisingly good understanding of the inner workings of the bank. He had a good awareness of banking procedures, cash flows, which staff were allies, which were not, and most other general gossip about people and their families.

"Afternoon, Mr Kheng. Did you see that the technicians came down from Khoyleng today? They put the new video cameras in. There are four of them dotted about the place. New-fangled technology. Waste of money of course."

Mr Tann made a 'hummph' kind of noise to further emphasise his displeasure with the 'new-fangled'.

"Cameras, Mr Tann?"

"Yes. One of Mr Hua Lin's latest ideas. It should be of interest to you though, Kheng. Extra security, you see. This is what Mr Hua Lin has been telling us all anyway. Look, one of them's up there on the side of the wall pointing at the gate. It sends a live picture to the computer inside Old Papa Han's office, sorry Hua Lin's office, so he can watch everything that's going on. He says it's how they do things in the capital, so we should do the same. It's the policy, we are told."

Kheng had already observed the arrival of the new technology before Mr Tann had felt obliged to point it out. However, to fain ignorance seemed a good way to draw Mr Tann into the conversation. Kheng had also assumed that the new manager was the driving force behind the change. After all, in the past seven years there had been no real changes at the bank at all, apart from Mr Hua Lin's arrival. The new security measures had all happened without any consultation. Kheng was a little put out by the lack of communication on this new investment. Particularly considering that he was technically the primary member of the bank's security team – if indeed the only person whose job was 100% dedicated to security.

Mr Hua Lin had organised for a support visit from the security technical team at head office. The security system with the closed-circuit cameras was a well-established initiative in Khoyleng but hadn't ever filtered down to Maklai, mainly because Papa Han had never requested it. Having arrived mid-morning and having made their presence known as important people from the central office, the city slickers had produced four security cameras, which had since been set up in strategic locations. Two were placed outside, with one of them screwed onto the corner of the building aimed at the front gate. Another peered down from near the guttering and was watching the front of the building, including the main entrance. Two more cameras were positioned inside the bank, monitoring the customers and cashiers as they moved money forward and back across the counters. Hua Lin wanted the bank staff to know that the lax days of Papa Han were well and truly behind them. They all had to follow bank procedures and policies now. The Maklai staff were judged to be an archaic institution from a provincial backwater, but all of that was about to change. Not only did that include doing the right thing, but it included being seen to do the right thing, and that included being seen on camera. Inside the manager's office was a new computer where the screen was divided into four squares, each one showing the action from a different security camera. Before the day was out the system was in place. The technical team had departed back to Khoyleng looking smug and feeling grateful that they had enough time to get back to the comforts of the capital without being stuck for the night in provincial Maklai. Mr Hua Lin was left to study various dull and uneventful angles of his bank from the confines of his office.

For Kheng, the advent of the security cameras would have two significant impacts. The first was that it was no longer possible for him to slip out through the front gate at night and go home for his dinner. Once everyone had gone home, he had been able to peer through the manager's office window and study the computer screen showing the view that was surveyed by the new technology. The only real way to get out of the compound unnoticed was to use his chair and put it up against the wall, right in the corner of the compound, as this part of the wall was not covered by the camera. He would then need to scramble to the top of the wall, and then climb down the small tree on the other side and onto the street. It was hardly convenient. Also, it meant that he still had to walk back, past the gates at the front of the bank which were now under surveillance, as his house was in the other direction to the climbable corner of the wall. Fortunately this was where the current ad-hoc road construction became a blessing in disguise.

As a result of enthusiastically starting the major construction project but not finishing any part of it, the provincial government had ensured that there was a comfortably sized and totally dry drainage tunnel passing straight in front of the bank. As Kheng had observed at the end of the rainy season, the small pipes for the inlets had been clogged with rubbish and mud after the first significant downpour, turning the roads into rivers and ensuring that the drains themselves were the driest place in the town. All he needed to do was hop inside the gap where eventually they would build a man-hole cover, crawl a few metres through the large concrete-ringed tunnel that had been laid across the entrance of the bank, and pop up again at the next future man-hole gap before continuing on his way. It was a bit inconvenient, but the first time he did this he took an old broom with him and swept the dust out from the pipes. Otherwise, it added less than two minutes to his usual dinnertime journey, and after all he wasn't bound by any particular schedule other than his wife's cooking plan.

The second inconvenience that the cameras brought was more psychological. They were very disempowering for Kheng. He felt like he had been diminished from the person that was respected and trusted to guard the provincial bank, to become someone that was being guarded himself. A computer was now basically considered more responsible for the security of the front gate than he was. Therefore, his motivation to be a dedicated member of the bank's team waned considerably, and his work attitude reverted to that of an employee that was untrusted, and should just clock in, do the minimum and pick up their pay. As a result of this disempowerment, Kheng's breaks for dinner started to become considerably longer than had previously been the case. Also, the added effort of negotiating the wall and the construction obstacle course left Kheng feeling compelled to stay at home even longer to have his dinner to justify the exertion. However, the new cameras were just the very start of it. It wouldn't be long before even more radical changes to the established security system would be introduced.

***

The day after the staff luncheon Mr Hua Lin had moved into Papa Han's office. He had spent his time reviewing procedures and meeting staff. The second day Mr Hua Lin had sat at Old Papa Han's desk, and scratched his head with despair in his attempt to eradicate the problem-induced itch. It didn't work.

Old Papa Han had had a reputation for being a bit archaic, and with this in mind Mr Hua Lin had accepted there would be a need to modernise a few things around the bank. He assumed there would be a need to make sure everyone was up to date on all of the bank's latest policies. He would need to ensure the procedures regarding data entry on the computing system were all being followed, back copies of ledgers were made, and that all methods for checking the balances were in place. However, he did not expect to find that the bank's security was so lax it was barely even guarded. There was one old man mooching around the compound at night. He had nothing but the chop sticks he ate his rice with to defend the bank in the face of a horde of thugs forcing open the gates. For Mr Hua Lin this didn't really count as an efficient system. Worse still, in the daytime there was no security at all. People were coming and going with money, cash was moving from the safe room to the bank tellers, and yet with all that the only security was a belief that nothing was likely to go wrong because nothing bad ever happened in Maklai. There was no continuity to the security system. If something went missing at night then the guard would simply claim that it had happened before he got to work when he couldn't be culpable. Besides, that would be a reasonable explanation. A daylight robbery was just as likely as a night time one. For a start, the door was already open, which would be of great advantage to any enthusiastic robbers, the clerks were moving around the cash, and the response time of the local police could be measured in days rather than hours. The risk for any would-be robber was minimal, so long as they wore a mask and weren't directly related to anyone at the bank that might recognise them. In fact, it would be considered to be more responsible to keep their relative out of trouble than to report them.

Lax security was one thing. A clear disregard of the labour law was yet another. The most that anyone could be asked to work on a weekly basis was forty-eight hours. If you added up the current quota of the old man who was doing the night guarding, he was probably clocking more than a hundred hours. This flouting of the law by such a well-respected institution had appalled Mr Hua Lin. It was totally unacceptable. If this type of disgrace found its way into the papers in Khoyleng the damage to the institution's reputation would be unimaginable. The damage to his reputation would be unacceptable. There was no way that Hua Lin was going to allow that kind of scandal on his watch. This provincial appointment was meant to be a stop gap career move to give him a boost up the Khoyleng ladder; it could not become the reason for him to slip down to the bottom. Mr Hua Lin had decided to take immediate action. Getting everyone to follow the standard procedures was a given. After that he would overhaul the bank's security system. He would then ensure his bank was following the letter of the law. That meant installing security cameras on the premises, and employing guards on eight hour shifts, each working less than forty-eight hours a week and with the right to annual leave. For this he would need a team of three regular guards and a relief guard. He began to plan the recruitment of the new team immediately, and started by drawing up a basic job description. The current guard would need one of these job descriptions as well. Hua Lin had gone through all the HR filing but it appeared that the guard had never been given one. How he had therefore been recruited in the first place was just one of the many mysteries that lingered with Hua Lin in the absence of Old Papa Han.

12. Interviewing

Mr Hua Lin had insisted on advertising the positions for the new guards almost immediately. By his second week in the job he was already interviewing candidates. The rapidity with which this took place was disconcerting for even the most forward thinking of the provincial bank's long-standing staff. The very smallest changes to the established routine would normally take weeks to months to take effect. A re-ordering of a whole section of staffing by week two of Hua Lin's arrival suggested that the new manager was ready to tear down everything and start again. Murmuring amongst colleagues about the new uncertainties became commonplace. Many were surprised that he'd not consulted the staff about this radical overhaul. Ordinarily, when institutions like the bank needed some bottom-feeder staff like cleaners or guards, then the word was put out amongst the staff to see who had a relative that would fit the bill. Usually someone had a brother-in-law who was looking for something to keep him occupied, or a sister who wanted some cleaning work now that the children were older. That way at least you knew the person came from a respectable family and it would help out an employee at the same time.

Hua Lin had devised a very clear recruitment process

with a very simple interview for the short-listed applicants to the position of guard. He had basically recognised it was very difficult to interview for the guard position. The talents that make someone a useful watchman for a sleepy provincial establishment are difficult to measure through direct questioning alone. An interview for a financial manager or clerk was quite different. For these skill-based jobs there were technical questions to be asked. Tests of the ability of a candidate to understand ledgers were straightforward. There were ways to assess appreciation of accountability. Example scenarios could be discussed to explore how to deal with problematic customers. A review of aptitude and ambition was a conversation that could be initiated. It was all very straightforward.

Guards, meanwhile, needed to be motivated by having very little to motivate them. They needed to be alert to the gentle passing of the meaningless and the benign. They had to be reliable at being awake when no one was watching. A day when nothing was achieved was a day when they achieved their task. It was a case of ensuring nothing out of the ordinary affected normality. In short, formulating a series of questions that could be posed to potential guards to assess their capacity in this regard was almost impossible. Indeed if such questions existed, and they were answered well, it would suggest that the aptitude of the applicant was far higher than the motivation that the position could bring. A mediocre answer was therefore better than a good one. Of course Mr Hua Lin was well aware that, with guards, the best way to identify a good one was through references. After all, the criteria of reliability, honesty, and good character were all part of a person's reputation. This was not measurable by a deft ability with clever answers when questioned in an interview. Unfortunately, the references that could be gathered in a small town like Maklai that would indicate a person's reputation were notably unreliable. They were usually from someone nominated by the applicant who was savvy enough to pick someone they were friendly with. Even if you bypassed their proposed list of character references and followed up with a village elder from their community, based on the address in their application, it would be very bad form for the elder to give a bad review. It wasn't the customary way. Besides, the implications of being less than complimentary about a member of your own community to some outsider were considerably greater than giving a glowing reference for someone who was known to be lazy and dishonest and went on to do a bad job. The consequence of being viewed by one random employer of being an unreliable witness to an applicant's character was a very minor concern compared with being responsible for someone in your community missing out on some gainful employment because of something you had said.

Despite the considerable obstacles to producing a definitive system of assessing the perfect guard, Hua Lin came up with a series of three questions. The first reviewed their previous work experience. The second asked if they understood what the daily duties of a guard might entail. The third, and perhaps most telling of the three, enquired what they imagined their response might be, in the middle of the night, if they came across a miscreant scaling the back wall of the bank in a first step towards breaking in and robbing the place. The first two questions would weed out a few of the less likely candidates. However, for Hua Lin, question three was the real test.

Eleven candidates had applied for the position and Mr Hua Lin had decided to interview all of them. After all, he needed to find three more guards if he was to conform to the national labour law and the bank's policy. Even interviewing all of them would only give him over a one in three chance of finding the right people. He decided that Mr Tann would join on the interview panel to provide some local knowledge and increase the impartiality of the process.

The first applicant to be interviewed was an elderly gentlemen. Hua Lin politely invited him into his office. He introduced himself and Mr Tann before proceeding to explain the interview process. It soon became very clear that the smiling grandfather sitting before him was not following a word that was said. Hua Lin motioned towards Mr Tann and provided a further introduction. The candidate leaned forward and slowly studied the face of Mr Tann before gradually lowering himself back down and releasing a loud and questioning grunt. From this Mr Hua Lin surmised that not only was it the hearing of the candidate that disqualified him from the guard position, but his failing eyesight as well. He immediately modified the recruitment process to include a basic pre-interview health inspection, where only those meeting minimum standards of functioning senses could proceed to the next level.

The newly imposed prerequisite seemed to weed out a number of hopefuls, but eventually Hua Lin was able to resume his process of identifying those candidates with notable strategic and critical thinking skills that they could apply in the event of a night time intruder.

The first health-checked applicant of the morning was a younger man who had just left high school. He answered question three by vowing that he would defend the compound with all his strength and fight the intruder to the death, with his bare hands if necessary.

The second applicant was a middle aged man with a

nervous laugh, who was clearly not used to being in a manager's room, and he shuffled uncomfortably in his chair throughout the process. Despite his fidgeting, he was more pragmatic than the high school graduate, and suggested he would hit the intruder with a gardening tool. At the end of the interview, Hua Lin asked him if he had any questions. The shuffler pointed out that his son was now a policeman who had been issued with a revolver but he very rarely used it. In fact he had no use for it at night at all and would happily lend it to him. Therefore, his question was, would he be allowed to bring the gun belonging to his son to work with him? If an intruder should scale the wall in the early hours then he would be well positioned to shoot him several times.

The third applicant was less fidgety but had a habit of tapping the table with his fingers at the start of each answer. He suggested that he would shine a torch at the intruder, challenge his presence and loudly sound the alarm.

After the third interview Mr Hua Lin asked Mr Tann what he thought of the candidates so far. Mr Tann had thought that the man with the son in the police force sounded like he could be quite useful, and was by far the most impressive of the three. Hua Lin did not agree. In fact he felt that the degree to which their opinions were not aligned was significant, and he found Mr Tann's observation a little concerning. The last thing they needed at the bank was the fatal shooting of some kid scaling the wall in an attempt to improve his chances of stealing the mangoes from the neighbour's overhanging tree. This might be all the more sensitive if the bullets came from a gun that was unofficially borrowed from a local police sergeant. He pointed this out to Mr Tann. Mr Tann countered his argument by explaining that the first man had a reputation in town for being hot-tempered, and the third one was well known for getting drunk. In fact he had seen him get drunk and pass out at the wedding of the district governor's nephew long before the karaoke had even got into full swing. Even with the risk of an accidental shooting with an illegally obtained firearm, the second candidate was still by far the best option of those they'd seen.

Mr Hua Lin decided that Mr Tann's judgement was even more questionable than that of the candidate that he was backing. He decided that he would do the interviews alone after that. He didn't want his recruitment to result in a murder on the bank's premises, followed by a complicated law suit that would inevitably focus on why the accused had been armed with a standard police-issue revolver.

By the end of the afternoon and several more interviews, two new guards and a relief guard had been identified. Contracts were drawn up the following day, and a shift system was applied, based on one they used in a neighbouring province's bank. Two days after the installation of the security cameras, Kheng was no longer the Maklai Provincial Bank night guard. He was now a shift-worker, one of a team.

13. Shift-Work

Shift-work didn't really suit Kheng, and he wasn't enjoying his first day of it. He was more of a 'be your own boss' and 'have the place to yourself' kind of person. Hua Lin had been in Papa Han's office less than two weeks and this was the result. Imagine what this place was going to be like a year from now.

Due to the new system, Kheng's working day had started at the unusual time of six o'clock in the morning and would end at two in the afternoon. It was all wrong. It meant he'd miss breakfast, and would then have a very late lunch, which would no doubt play havoc with his digestive system. It would probably mean that he wouldn't be properly hungry at dinnertime either. Apart from the meal side of things, it would also result in his being at home in the afternoon and he would get under his wife's feet. Worse, he would still be there in the evening, which is when his wife liked to sit up talking with her cronies and hooting unnecessarily loudly at the day's gossip. Normally she did this with her neighbour Mama Tae, or sometimes with one of her relatives if they came round to visit in the evening. If Kheng was there, she always started talking at him and wanted to make him be part of the incessant rattling. Over the years he'd forgotten to cherish the advantage that his night-job gave him in that regard.

Another sticking point with the morning shift was that Kheng would have to be present and awake for most of the time. Unlike when doing the night guarding, during the day the boss and the other bank workers were all there as well, so he couldn't just laze around in a hammock any more.

When the new shift system had been introduced, Mr Hua Lin had explained to Kheng that at the end of each shift Kheng was expected to hand over responsibility of the bank's compound's security to the next guard. This would involve passing on the guarding equipment, which was essentially a torch and charger. They then had to do a circuit of the grounds to check nothing was missing or suspicious, and note this down in the new guards' handing-over book, along with their names, the date and the time, before both guards signed it.

At 2pm Kheng watched with trepidation as the new guard cautiously wandered through the bank's aging gates and made his way towards him. By Kheng's estimation the man was probably in his late fifties. However, once men like him reached a certain age it was difficult to tell. One lined and world-weary face was very much like the next. It was more appropriate to switch to an epoch-based classification of age rather than continue with the regular monitoring of progress with measurable years.

"I'm the new guard. Meebor they call me."

Kheng acknowledged his presence with a subtle nod.

"I'm Kheng. I'm supposed to hand over the shift-work to you using this notebook."

Meebor nodded sagely back at him.

"They said something about that when I signed the contract. That young guy from the city kept going on about accountability or some such nonsense. I can write a bit. Mostly my name and numbers, stuff like that. I'm not so hot with longer sentences. Let's hope there's not too much to check."

Kheng led Meebor on a two minute tour of the bank's acreage, carefully noting the presence of the old plastic chair which he had now positioned so he could sit dutifully by the gate to reassure the customers of their safety. Other items of note were the padlock and key for the gate and the absence of any suspicious ropes, tunnelling equipment or getaway cars that might imply a major heist was under way. Kheng also pointed out to Meebor the security camera situation, and they quietly peered through the window of Mr Hua Lin's office so Meebor could see what they did. As they returned to the front of the bank, Meebor concluded the handover with an astute observation.

"That camera on the gate's a problem. It's not going to be easy for me to go and have dinner, and I've not brought anything with me."

"Your wife could bring you something."

Kheng offered an alternative, noting that Meebor didn't seem to be searching his mind too actively for his own solution.

"She's not the sort of wife that would offer to walk down here and bring food to me. She's more the sort of wife that would nag me for asking in the first place."

Kheng nodded sympathetically. He too had never had the courage to suggest to his wife that it would be helpful to courier some nourishment over to him while he was at work. There would be a million good reasons why it was not possible. A major one would be that the benefits of Kheng's not being at home and getting under her feet would be totally diluted by her having to leave the home during that period of calm because of him.

Kheng had decided that he was sympathetic to

Meebor's domestic problems. They shared a down trodden kindred spirit.

"Let's go and look at the computer screen again through the window."

Kheng decided that he would show Meebor how the camera for the gate didn't capture the far corner of the wall where you could climb over and then use the newly installed part-built empty drainage system next to the road to get past the gate. It wasn't a detail that he'd planned to be part of the guard handover notebook system. However, as it was apparent that Meebor wasn't much of a writer, there was no real risk that any record of it was going to end up in the journal by accident.

14. Unlucky Numbers

Nelea and Mama Tae had invested significantly in the lucky numbers that they had extracted from Kheng's dream. Particularly by Nelea's standards, as she didn't always do the lottery quite as religiously as Mama Tae. They'd each bought ten tickets using different combinations of the numbers for different games. When nothing came up they went back the next day and did the same. Despite their unwavering commitment to the interpretation of Kheng's vision, none of the numbers had come up. Over the last week Mama Tae and Nelea had spent several afternoons enjoying a pipe and going back through the details of the dream, looking for any glimmer of a number that had been missed. After considerable scrutiny they could find no errors in the interpretation. The dream was so fantastic that it must mean something numerical. Mama Tae arrived at the conclusion that the problem lay with the raw information itself. It was time to haul Mr Kheng and his dream spirits back to the fireplace and revisit every aspect of this vision of his. Clearly there was something he wasn't sharing, or a detail he'd overlooked.

Kheng reluctantly sat before the fire. It was his first post-shift afternoon and as predicted his new availability in the house was immediately impacting negatively on his simple but pleasant way of life. Once more he suffered the ash clouds that trailed behind Mama Tae's flamboyant and exuberant arms as she drew herself into a trance before him. He already regretted sharing his vision once with the manic rattan furniture sales woman, and now he regretted it even more. All this theatre was also encouraging his normally sensible wife down an increasingly deviating path.

"Mr Kheng…"

Mama Tae fluttered her eyes upward so that they were mostly completely white, like in the movies when someone is pretending to be possessed. Kheng wondered how this addition to proceedings would sway the opinion of any fence-sitting dream spirits and help them consider the ritual as something that was worth engaging in after all.

"Mr Kheng, recant onto us once more you dream story."

"I've told you all of it last time. Perhaps we should give it a rest."

Kheng also wondered why calling on the presence of dream spirits required a deviation from the normal way of saying words. Mama Tae snapped out of her reverie and glared sternly at Kheng.

"The details, Kheng. Now."

Mama Tae returned to her trance like state as if her sudden return to clarity had never taken place. She started to take deep and noisy breaths to add to the drama of her heightened state. Kheng decided it would be quicker in the long run just to play along.

"Like I said before, there was a large orange moon, filled with hot liquid gold. It rose from behind a big old tree and then the pig said all the weird stuff about triangles and buffaloes before Aunt Kayla appeared out of nowhere looking miserable, and then I woke up."

Mama Tae dropped out from her trance and returned to being an angry neighbour again.

"Kheng! You need to take this seriously or we will keep going until you do. Now, from the beginning and with proper description and details this time."

"Wait!"

It was Nelea's turn to become animated.

"Wait, Mama Tae. Kheng just said the moon rose up from behind a large tree. He didn't tell us that bit last time. There was no mention of a big tree before. That's the missing piece of the puzzle."

"You're right, Nelea. The tree is the missing piece. Look at the time and money we've wasted because we couldn't add in the tree number to the lottery. Kheng, I hope you're learning from this. The trouble and expense you've put your poor wife to."

Mama Tae was most definitely in a post-trance state by now and becoming quite excitable. Kheng decided to respond with his own frustration:

"You didn't add a number for Aunt Kaylin either."

Kheng was a bit fed up. He failed to see how any of this was his fault. He'd never been particularly up for the dream interpretation in the first place. If they were going to be selective about which bits they wanted to assign to the numbers to, then that was hardly his concern. However, Mama Tae was never going to let Kheng get the last word:

"How can a dream summon up a number for your Aunt Kaylin. Don't be so ridiculous. Honestly, I don't know how poor Nelea copes I really don't."

Kheng accepted the scolding from Mama Tae and didn't take the argument further. However, he could think of various ways to numerically describe an aunt. The number of aunts that you have; the age of the aunt in question; the number of functioning teeth belonging to the aunt. These were just three examples of many.

Nelea dragged them back to the vital question:

"So what does the tree mean? And what number does the tree give us then?"

Mama Tae took a deep breath and transformed herself back to the sage oracle of dream interpretation.

"Trees can mean anything really. The roots are the past, the trunk is the present and the branches the future. It depends a lot on the type of tree and what it was up to at the time. Was it a flowering tree? A dead tree? A very branchy tree? Were the leaves doing anything notable? Were there lots of gnarly bits of bark suggesting it was a very old tree? Was there anything in the tree like a big menacing bird or a dinosaur or an old pair of shoes, or a sack of rice?"

"It was just a big old tree. Just for a moment at the beginning. After that I was focused on the moon and the tree was gone."

"Well, it's probably irrelevant then to the overall interpretation. But you really must pay more attention next time. Who knows what important stuff we could all be missing out on. Anyway, the brevity of the tree or what it looked like doesn't affect the numbers. Trees are usually a number four. That should be obviously clear to anyone who insists on dreaming about things."

Nelea seemed less certain with the outcome of this.

"Well, we had number four anyway. Four was also the strength number."

She gave this some thought before starting to cheer up a little.

"However,…with four being represented more strongly that we thought then it means we have to put it as the first number for the different lottery combinations."

Mama Tae gave Nelea's explanation due consideration.

"You may be right. That does make a lot of sense. We'd better head off to town and have another go at the lottery then."

Kheng watched them leave. At least the dream had provided one thing: the house to himself for a few hours. He took his hammock out of his work-bag, tied it between two of the posts beneath his stilted home and settled in for a late afternoon nap.

15. Salt

Kheng had understood that he would have a week of doing the morning shift. He would then be rotated to the afternoon shift. The other two guards would rotate as well. The fourth guard would be available later on to cover for sick leave and the annual leave, a policy which had now been introduced. Mr Hua Lin had explained that this meant that the bank was now responsibly and proudly upholding the country's labour law. Kheng took his word for it. Sadly the country's generous labour laws were very much disturbing a routine that Kheng had been quite comfortable with in his ignorance.

When Kheng arrived at 6am the next morning to start his shift he was greeted by the new night guard who was finishing off his first shift on the job.

"Good morning Mr Kheng."

"Good morning. Errr?"

"Salt. Everyone calls me Salt. Even my wife. Her idea in fact. I always put too much salt on my food. She says I ruin it. That or MSG. But you can't call someone MSG now, can you?"

"I guess not."

Kheng smiled in agreement. He decided he would be unable to dispute such a wise observation about food additives, even at a reasonable hour of the day.

"Thanks for the tip about the camera, Kheng. Old Mr Meebor passed it on. Very handy for nipping home. Popped back and got a flask of coffee. When you were on nights, where did you sleep? I tried sleeping in the chair. It's playing havoc with my back this morning."

Kheng decided he vaguely knew this Salt. Something about the way he talked. Maybe he'd been in the army as well. However, it was very early in the morning and he was in no mood for a reunion with someone he wasn't sure he knew.

"Have you got the handing-over book with you, Mr Salt?"

Salt waved the already dog-eared student notebook aloft to demonstrate that he had.

"Got it right here, Mr Kheng. Shall we do the handover now, or do you want coffee? There's still some in the flask. Don't know where we'll both sit though. Only one chair. Only one cup as well, actually. I'll have to remember an extra one tomorrow. Or you could bring one."

Salt poured Kheng some coffee in the solitary cup, and Kheng took a sip whilst carefully studying the handing-over note book. It was already becoming quite repetitive and there had only been two handovers so far. Both records of the shift handover recognised that the chair had remained an asset and that it was not lost to the institution despite the various staff responsible for it. The same could be said for the torch and charger. Meanwhile nothing untoward had gone on beyond the concerns of the limited furniture.

"Thanks for the coffee, Mr Salt. It was good."

"Not too salty then, eh? Sorry. Family joke. My wife always says that, if I say something was nice. Can't win really. Damned either way."

Kheng made a sympathetic noise and decided he didn't

begrudge Mr Salt the current loss of his night shift to him one bit. Salt's wife sounded like a nightmare. His wife nagged, but at least she hadn't renamed him after a type of condiment and then laid into him about it all the time. He decided to help out his new colleague with the sleeping dilemma.

"I used to bring a hammock to work with me in my bag. I packed it beneath a food container so it looked like I'd just brought dinner. There's a tree at the back and a hook I put in the old wall. They are the right distance apart to hang the hammock comfortably between the two. Fortunately there are no new security cameras around the back, so it shouldn't be a problem. I'll show you before I leave."

Kheng handed back the empty cup, and folded the handover book so it could fit in his pocket. He led Salt around to the rear of the building to show him how to set up the hammock. Kheng was surprising himself at how quickly he was surrendering all the tricks of his trade. Firstly the storm pipe system at the front of the bank to dodge the camera, and now the hammock. However, Kheng had to face that things were very different now. Before Hua Lin arrived he'd thought of himself as one of the bank employees. Now there were white collar day workers and blue collar shift workers. He was one of the latter. New alliances were a necessity. The cameras were the real security for the bank, and he had a social responsibility to make sure these new recruits understood the ropes so they didn't compromise their jobs. It sounded like the trouble they would both be in with their wives would be horrendous if they did.

After the hammock hook inspection, Mr Salt made his way out of the compound leaving Kheng to take charge. Kheng positioned himself at the front of the office, so that he could feign the pretence of an eager and well-disciplined guard for when the new boss arrived. It also fitted with Kheng's ongoing obsession of monitoring the road work progress. The construction workers would begin in about an hour's time and so he positioned the chair near the gate so he would be ready for the start of proceedings. Earlier in the week, on the opposite side of the street, they'd started putting together the form-work for the drainage inspection hatches. Not quite as interesting as when the big rollers and back hoes were trundling back and forth, but an interesting side-activity for him as he followed the overall process.

At about twenty to eight Mr Tann walked up to the gate and produced his keys from his satchel. Ms Win-Kham was striding up to the gate right behind him. Kheng had noticed that there had been a subtle change in the routine for both of these employees over recent days. Normally, Mr Tann would pop up at about eight o'clock or a bit after and open up the bank. The other staff would drift in over the following half an hour or so. Kheng usually passed a number of them on the street as he walked home. Since the change of management had taken place, Ms Win-Kham has started dead-heating with Mr Tann at the front of the bank exactly on eight o'clock, with Mr Hua Lin arriving shortly afterwards. This had clearly unnerved the old man who had understood that one of his few duties was to make sure that he was the first to arrive and have things open and ready for the boss. In response, he had started arriving five minutes earlier, and, strangely, so did Ms Win-Kham. It was all highly irregular. Particularly as Ms Win-Kham seemed to be more smartly dressed these days in more expensive tailored suits and wearing heels. It was a wonder she could get down the street at all, especially with all the drainage works going on, let alone make it in early.

Having played the game of who could arrive first for some time now, and taking gradual bites into the pre-eight o'clock time slot, Mr Tann and Ms Win-Kham were now running about twenty minutes ahead of the normal schedule. In the old days this would have worked out well for Kheng, as once Mr Tann had taken charge of the premises he could go home. However, with the new shift work in place Mr Tann's arrival time was becoming wholly irrelevant. Let alone that of Ms Win-Kham.

16. Ms. Win-Kham

Ms Win-Kham had done reasonably well for herself. She was quite young when she achieved the status of head cashier at the provincial bank. Well, young by Maklai standards anyway. She had a steady job, a steady salary, and a small home, for which she was always able to pay the rent on time. Meanwhile, she was entering her early thirties and her looks were still holding, should she ever need to call on them. Due to the slow pace of Maklai life and lack of interesting opportunities, Ms Win-Kham had concluded for some time that there was very little reason to call on either her looks or her intellect to support any attempts at self-improvement.

The interests of her more recent local suitors had rarely extended beyond their own ambitions for self-betterment in Maklai. They were primarily attracted to Win-Kham because she clearly had a steady income, to which they would have full access once the monks had made their blessings. The potential husbands either wanted to marry a woman with a well-paid job so that they wouldn't have to get one of their own, or so that they had more money to pay for their drinking. Social progression for men in Maklai meant getting drunk with a slightly higher level of business or administrative stratum than you previously aspired to get drunk with. The marginal economics of cronyism then gradually played out. Nobody really tried to dream big.

Ms Win-Kham looked back on her dalliances with the opposite sex as rather un-inspirational. Until now, and much to her mother's disappointment, the lack of sensible options had caused Win-Kham to remain staunchly independent and single. She had intelligence and ambition. She wasn't going to compromise her success and achievement to settle for a man from Maklai who would expect multiple children and her undying patience and acceptance when he either came home drunk or not at all. She wasn't saving herself for love, but she was saving herself for a better opportunity. That opportunity might just be the new manager of the Maklai bank and his navy blue tie.

In Mr Hua Lin, Ms Win-Kham saw a man with ambition. He was like her, looking for a way to get up a ladder that had been designed for someone with better connections than his own. Men with ambition didn't stick around for long in places like Maklai. Soon enough they gravitated back to their socially-charged lives in the big city. It was rare for someone from the capital to come out to the provinces, which already made Hua Lin stand out in terms of his ambitions, but also, for the astute observer like Ms Win-Kham, it showed his vulnerability and lack of connections. Ms Win-Kham would need to make sure that when Hua Lin did eventually achieve his goal and return to the city for the next rung on the ladder of his career, her claws were sunk in deep enough to ensure she was carried back with him. She knew better than to assume she would be able to seduce him. People like Hua Lin had been to enough Khoyleng parties to know what their options were, both in terms of girlfriends and marriage. Girlfriends were for fun, and marriage was a financial investment to bring together influential families or build businesses. Ms Win-Kham was too old to be in the first category and insufficiently enriched in social standing and wealth to enable her to qualify for the second. However, there were other means of getting what she wanted. She would start by gaining his trust. This would be the beginning of a relationship between them, and by whatever means available she would become indispensable to him. Like a piece of particularly stringy chicken from a cling-film wrapped plate at the Sou-Rehn restaurant and the gap between her upper left incisors, the two would eventually become inseparable.

17. Meehor

By 2pm Kheng was quite looking forward to the arrival of Mr Meebor. He was starting to develop a strong sense of camaraderie with the new team. It was all very friendly. Kheng had begun to feel important, like he was the senior guard, handing down his wealth of experience to the new blood. He'd always cherished the solitude that the job had given him over the past years. This was particularly the case after the lack of privacy from the communal life of soldiering through his career, interspersed with the chaos of a large family. After his time in the army he'd appreciated the opportunity of some solitude to regroup a little and come to terms with some of the emotional stresses that the conflict had left him with. However, after seven years of quiet time, the new guarding system had added a new dimension and a bit of human interaction to his routine without it having to get too out of hand. He was on the brink of appreciating the arrival of Mr Hua Lin to their quiet little town and providing him with this new social element in his life.

Meebor sauntered through the gates at about ten past the hour, and gave a cheery wave as he did so.

"Afternoon, Mr Kheng."

"Afternoon, Mr Meebor. How did it all go yesterday?"

"Good, Mr Kheng. Very good. That thing with the storm drain is a handy little manoeuvre. Reminds me of the days when I used to be a burglar. I was always crawling through gaps in fences, holes in the eaves of people's roofs, under chicken coops with a small saw so I could make a hole in the floor and reach through to steal the eggs. You never get those wonderful days of your youth back again, do you, Mr Kheng? It's the price of getting older, that's what they say."

Meebor stretched out his arm so he could lean against the wall of the bank and let out a deep sigh as he wallowed in his reverie.

"That is quite true, Mr Meebor. It's only when we get older that we realise these things are passing us by."

Kheng tried to add a slightly surprised tone to his voice but not too much. The surprise was not for his new awareness of Meebor's criminal past, but more at how freely Meebor wanted to talk about it with someone he barely knew. There was a limit to how much Kheng really wanted to know, and that limit had already been crossed. There were certain things that Kheng was happy to be ignorant about.

"Of course it's been a while since I did anything like that, Mr Kheng. All that thieving and carry on. The wife would beat me to within an inch of my life if she thought I'd started up again. It's all very well for the family when the burglaring is going to plan and no one catches up with you. Once you're put away inside for a bit it's then much harder on them. The wife had to work all hours to make ends meet when I was locked up in the slammer, and she has never let me forget it. Anyways, it seems that's all far behind me now. Looks like I've finally landed a good honest job."

Kheng was not particularly surprised by this new and

openly shared information from his colleague. The modern history in their country of Feiquon had seen its share of tough and volatile times. Sometimes people did what they had to if they wanted to make it through, if only to find enough to eat. You can't always keep playing a straight die if the whole game is already rigged against you.

"So did Mr Hua Lin ask you about your past when he hired you?"

"No, not really. Well, yes. At times. Although he was mostly obsessing about thieves climbing the walls. But for my history, I made up a bit of the answers, and then focused more about the time I'd worked at the saw mill. I decided not to bring up the years in prison unless he specifically asked me a prison question. No specific questions about time in prison came up in the interview. He asked me to give the number for a reference of someone that I knew who he'd think was responsible. I gave a few, and then he phoned up Mr Videt the village head from our part of town. However, the old man is a relative of my wife, so he would never say anything bad to stop the family getting some income. Anyway, it's not as if I ever killed anyone or anything like that. If having a criminal record for that sort of thing counted against you, it'd be more of a surprise that they gave Mr Salt the job. Mind you, he did his time, sixteen years they say, so now he deserves a clean slate the same as the rest of us. Look out. That's Mr Navey. I see he's back in again, making another deposit. Twice in two days that is. He must be making some serious money."

"Sorry, what do you mean?"

"Well, I guess it's the ol' burglar in me. But sitting here, watching who are coming and going from the bank, how often they are here, how well they are dressed, their jewellery, what they drive. Well, within a few weeks I'll have a pretty good profile of everyone in town worth stealing from. I'll know who's got enough cash on them to be using the bank a lot, what days they get their money out, when would be a good time to break in to their house. You know, that sort of thing. Lucky for them I've gone straight really. Anyway, it passes the time."

Kheng's request for extra information had been more aimed at the 'Mr Salt' element of the conversation. The reference to Salt's sixteen years inside was intriguing. However, he decided to let it go. He'd never been one for gossip. That was his wife's job and it soon became very tedious. It was as well not to prise out gossip about one of your colleagues with other members of the team. Mr Salt would no doubt tell him about it eventually, if he wanted him to know.

"Anyway, Mr Kheng. I see the plastic chair is still here. You've got the torch? It was handy for getting through the concrete pipes on the way to dinner yesterday evening."

Kheng handed over the torch, noted down the subtle shift of responsibility for the valuable items in the text book, and then handed that over to Meebor as well.

"We'll take the patrol of the compound as read then, Mr Kheng?"

Kheng shrugged.

"Why not?"

After all, Kheng was rapidly learning that there was already a far higher percentage of the criminal underworld being paid to stay inside the compound of the bank than would ever be on the outside trying to get in.

18. The Evening Shift

A week after the new shift-work was introduced, Kheng was moved to the afternoon–evening time slot. Meebor got the early shift and Salt had stayed on the night shift. Mr Hua Lin had explained about some employment law about sleep deprivation so that night shift workers had to have the same routine for four weeks. It made very little sense to Kheng, especially with the knowledge that the night shift was having very little impact on anybody's sleeping pattern. However, the move to the afternoons would be a pleasant change for a number of reasons, so he didn't make a fuss. Firstly the hours were more sociable with no early starts or being out all night. For social interaction, it was the best of both worlds as there were a couple of hours in the afternoon when people were around, and then when the bank closed at four he had the place to himself. Surprisingly, a third reason that he was pleased to get the afternoon shift was to get the evening update from Mr Tann. Kheng had spent a week of providing the morning weather forecast, but had completely missed out on Mr Tann's afternoon summary of the latest news. Meebor had been on the afternoon shift, but had been fairly ineffectual at extracting interesting closing time information from the head clerk. Any titbits he did glean were then edited down for Mr Salt, who would forget most of it by the next morning for Kheng's third-hand news. It was therefore with a high degree of enthusiasm that Kheng greeted Mr Tann outside the door of the bank.

"Afternoon, Mr Tann. It's been a while since I said that. This shift-work is quite a change, modernisation, eh? How's everything at the bank today?"

"Oh, don't ask…"

Mr Tann sighed deeply. Kheng patiently stood by and watched the aging clerk rifle through the keys to find the one that locked the main door. Kheng knew that whenever someone says 'don't ask' it means they are probably desperate for you to patiently listen so they can unburden their soul to you.

"Mr Hua Lin is following the 'regulations' again."

Kheng listened attentively knowing there was more to come.

"He says every provincial branch of the bank is supposed to have a minimum amount of cash on hand. It's in the rule book from Khoyleng headquarters that we're all supposed to follow. That way, if there is a big event or a festival or we're cut off by flooding or something then we won't run out of money and disappoint the customers. It's supposed to help to make sure that we don't lose any important clients. Problem is of course that we don't have space for that much cash. The safe is twenty-five years old. One of the ones with the combination lock and the thick metal doors. Ol' Papa Han had it installed a few years after he started, and the only people who used the bank in those days were the government departments. We just don't have the space. We've got cash sitting around on the floor in bags next to the safe because we can't fit them inside, for goodness' sake!"

Mr Tann shook his head with a 'what dark days are

these' expression. Kheng responded with a similar act of mimicked despair.

"Anyway, Mr Tann. Nearly the weekend now."

"Is it? My brother's coming to visit at the weekend. Damn. His wife has the most annoying laugh. I think she's a bit simple minded. Annoying. Can you imagine the amount of paperwork it takes to order a new safe from head office, and all the signatures to get the request approved. They want to see a 'design' as well as the request document. It'll be weeks before we get this sorted out!"

With that Mr Tann shuffled out of the bank and wobbled his way across the bridge of planks that traversed the concrete storm drains that were still patiently waiting for the road team to return and bury them properly.

Kheng watched him go. He could see his frustration. Change was all well and good but sometimes patience was called for. It was something young men like Mr Hua Lin didn't always appreciate.

19. Important Clients

Mr Hua Lin had initially assumed that Papa Han, his predecessor, had been a redundant part of the furnishings in the bank for much of his tenure. However, now that he had been in the job for a few weeks, Hua Lin was gradually beginning to appreciate that Old Papa Han had subtly contributed to the bank in a way that Hua Lin was struggling to do. It was not through anything specific that the old man had actually done of course. It was more about who he was. He was 'old school'. Hua Lin was becoming increasingly aware of the value that being part of the establishment held in a small province like Maklai. Papa Han had been running the bank for twenty-something years, and had been working there for even longer. His family had always been influential in the town. As a younger man, Papa Han had transferred from the bank to serve in the army. As soon as a degree of normality had returned to the country, the provincial authorities had rewarded Papa Han's service with the position of manager at the provincial bank. Of course it was completely government-run back in those days. Recruitment was all about connections. Papa Han had got his job based on his community standing, his war record, and the connections and the respect that he had developed. He had then run the bank based on the same principles. Even though new banks had appeared in recent years, the high-rolling clients in the province stayed with the Khoyleng Bank because Papa Han was, and always had been, one of them. The management in Khoyleng had failed to appreciate the full value of this in a place like Maklai, and Mr Hua Lin was only just starting to understand as well.

In the short time that Hua Lin had been in charge a couple of important clients had already taken their money elsewhere. Now that loyalty, shared history, family connections and nationalistic camaraderie were less of a priority, high interest rates took precedence. Mr Hua Lin's managers in Khoyleng had expressed their concern at the loss of these highly important customers. They had sternly instructed him to get control over the problem of the diminishing loyalty of the long standing clientele, and to start looking after the bank's interests.

The strategy for pursuing loyalty in Maklai was not a complicated one. However, it did take time and resources. Mr Hua Lin found that he was taking important clients out for drinks most evenings in his efforts to entertain and garner respect. This inevitably meant ending up in karaoke bars until the early hours as there were very few nightlife options in Maklai. Hua Lin wasn't unaccustomed to burning the candle at both ends whilst in the capital, but that was with his mates, not as work. To gain influential friends and forge alliances in Maklai he had to be both sozzled and retain an unblemished reputation at the same time. It was all quite exhausting. There were no early nights when you were taking out important businessmen on drinking binges, and he still had to come in each morning and manage the bank.

It was a constant fight to perform his day job adequately

whilst impressing the top brass in Khoyleng with his client management. It meant that he was living well beyond his means, and was rapidly eating into his meagre savings considerably. He calculated that his finances could maintain the lavish, if undesired, lifestyle for about another three weeks before he was totally bankrupt. To his credit, Mr Hua Lin had managed to befriend a number of the provincial elite that held some of the bigger accounts at the bank, but this was small by comparison with the number he would need on his side to ensure the bank maintained its client base. He was starting to panic a little. The cushy little side step to the provinces to boost his career was not playing out as he had hoped.

To address the duel challenges of sleep deprivation and bankruptcy, Hua Lin decided that he had two choices. The first was to fast track his way into Maklai provincial society. The traditional route for this option was to court an available daughter of one of the bigger account holders with government influence. A recently come of age unspoken for young woman would need to be identified and then pursued relentlessly. However, this was a long-term plan in relation to his rapidly dwindling finances. He would need considerable capital in order to impress such an eligible young lady and convince her that he was of an equal standing. His gifts and exuberant gestures were not only expected by her but by the parents as well if he was to show he had what it took to be a prominent man in an extended family.

The second option was to seek additional money without having to marry it. He didn't want a loan, interest rates were high, even if you worked at the bank. Also, he didn't want his bosses to see that he was struggling to manage his own money, let alone that of the bank. There was certainly no way he could go and borrow money from a rival bank in Maklai. That would destroy any reputation that he'd worked so hard to build. What he needed was some kind of benefactor, or a piece of incredibly good luck. It seemed crazy that he could be in charge of so much money at the bank, and yet working for that same bank was rapidly spiralling him into poverty. Ideally the bank should be paying for his expenses when entertaining the clients. However, that was an argument that he would never win. Papa Han had never needed to claim vast expenses to keep hold of their big accounts. If Hua Lin now claimed it was necessary, then the management in Khoyleng would just conclude they'd picked the wrong man for the job.

20. Mr. Salt's Wife

Mr Salt was nearly an hour late when he finally rolled up at the gates of the provincial bank to relieve Kheng of his evening shift. Kheng didn't mind too much, but it was nearly 11pm. If, for the next week he had the chance of both sleeping in his bed but being home late enough to miss out on his wife gossiping with the loopy rattan seller from next door, then he wanted to get back home in time and make the most of it.

"Sorry I'm so late, Mr Kheng. Been at the hospital all day. Wife's in there. Not well at all. Problem with her blood."

"Not to worry, Mr Salt. There are always going to be family issues that come up and have to be put first. Sit yourself down on the chair and get your breath back a while."

"Doctors want to keep her in. Maybe she has to stay for weeks. Doctors were talking about her kidneys. Said they would need to use expensive machines. We can't afford expensive machines. She's not working of course. Just me. I don't know what we'll do. We've got no money, other than what we live on. I can just about afford to keep her in overnight. We'll struggle to pay for the next few days. I can't pay for her to stay after that. Let alone pay for any expensive machines. It's not good, Mr Kheng. Not good at all."

"What about your family. Can they help?"

"We've got no relatives. Well, not with any money. None that we keep in touch with. None that stay in touch with us anyway. The boy's a hopeless layabout. My girl's still in high school. We started our family quite late you see. I was, well, 'away'."

Kheng nodded. He was intrigued why there was no extended family for Mr Salt to fall back on in his time of need. The extended family was an inevitable part of life, sometimes to your benefit, sometimes not, but they were always there. The story behind why Mr Salt had been 'away' for much of his middle-years also raised Kheng's curiosity, but now probably wasn't the time to dig into that one. It seemed the problem with his wife needed to be addressed first.

"I'll help you get your hammock set up and you have a bit of a lie down and get your head straight. There's always a way with these things if you put your mind to it. After all, you can't stop her treatment if she needs it, so a solution will have to present itself."

Mr Salt watched as Kheng put up the hammock, regretting that he'd arrived in too much of a fluster to remember to bring any coffee.

"There that should do."

Kheng straighten his back, and picked up his rucksack.

"Oh, and here. Make your mark in the handover book to say that you've got the chair and the torch."

Kheng passed over the notebook and watched as Salt scrawled his name next to where Kheng had written 'torch' and 'chair'.

"What about getting a loan, Mr Salt? After all you are an employee at the bank now. Maybe they can do you a good rate?"

"Already asked Mr Tann. He wasn't impressed. Sceptical that I was trying to get perks. It is my first month at the job. Said that I could get an advance of half a month's salary. Got to come out of the next pay though – so doesn't make a lot of difference. They won't give much of a loan. They know how much they pay me. And how old I am. This isn't something I can put off for a few weeks. She needs help now. She might die, Mr Kheng."

Salt slumped back in the hammock and gazed at the stars as the leaves of the jackfruit tree rustled in the breeze and intermittently provided a brief view of the night sky. Despair had overtaken his ability to think straight about any of it.

Kheng tried to talk it through.

"Well there must be a way. Other people have to get treatment at the hospital. They can hardly turn your wife away now, not if she really needs help."

"Well, if you come up with something, Mr Kheng, then let me know. I'm at my wits end. I can't lose her you know. Not now. Not with so much time lost already."

Kheng headed out into the night, carefully negotiating the wobbly planks over the pipe-filled trench as he did so. Fortunately the moon was starting to wax larger and so there was enough light to see where to tread. Poor Mr Salt was in a fix all right. Somehow families usually rallied and came up with a solution. It sounded like Mr Salt didn't have the support. It was unusual not to have an extended family at times of need, even close neighbours from the village were often happy to help out at a time like this. If none of those avenues existed then he really might be in trouble. No money would mean no treatment. It was clear that Mr Salt's wife needed help straight away.

21. Kheng's Dream

Kheng woke up with a start. It had been a puzzling, almost disturbing dream. More so, because it was the exact same dream that had affected him so much earlier in the month. This was significant. Even Kheng with his sceptical approach to fortune telling could see that. Normally he could never recall what he had dreamt beyond that brief period of being half asleep and half wake. Almost immediately the clarity was lost to him like the evaporation of an early morning mist as the rising sun began to burn away the cool lingering remains of the night. All he would be left with was the knowledge of images that he could no longer recall.

Unusually, as with the last time this dream had happened to him, the images and clarity had very much stuck with him. It might have been because he was sleeping at home next to his wife instead of in his hammock at the bank. He liked his hammock and always got a good sleep. A night spent on a thin mattress on a wooden bed, and you might as well just sleep on the floor. He was always having to reposition himself to try and get his back comfortable. He never started the next day feeling refreshed like he did from the hammock. Maybe he'd remembered the dream because he'd not been quite as asleep as he normally was.

In Kheng's recurring dream the moon had appeared before him from behind the enormous tree. Just as before the full moon had shone with an incredible intensity and Kheng had known that it was made from liquid gold. Some of the molten gold had dripped down from the sky and landed on him, splashing on his skin. Kheng knew that it should have been white hot, but it didn't hurt, it just made him warm. Then from nowhere a large wild boar had appeared in front of the moon and faced Kheng with a gleam in its eye. It snorted a bit before announcing with a very well spoken but urgent voice: "The buffalo is a triangle. It's a triangle I'm telling you!" After that the pig vanished and Kheng's Aunt Kaylin had appeared from behind the moon with a scowl across her lined and cruel face. Waving her bamboo stick, she ordered him to go to the market to buy her whisky, and there'd be trouble if he came home without any. It was at that point that Kheng woke up once again in a cold sweat.

It was frustrating. More than that, it was troubling. It felt like there was more to come, to bring all the threads together and make sense, but he was waking up before the important part. Like watching a movie when you're about find out who the killer is but then the electricity goes off or the DVD is too scratched to get any further.

He really hoped that his Aunt Kaylin wasn't speaking to him from the grave. She had been terrifying enough when she was alive, but the arrival on the scene of Aunt Kaylin in spectral form didn't bear thinking about. It might just be that this new shift-work thing was putting his sleeping pattern out of kilter and making him restless. It could take a while to get back to normal sleep with that sort of thing going on. Besides, Mr Salt's family problems had caused him to be even later in getting home. It had been midnight by the time he eventually got to bed.

Another option was that there could also be some kind of malicious spirit playing tricks with his mind. He'd spent a lot of time on patrol in the depths of the forests when he was in the army, pitching camp amongst the undergrowth, trekking for days through the jungles to scout the enemy. He could well have been inadvertently collecting up spirits as he made his way through the dense forest. They might have been clinging on like the spiny seeds from the grasses that attach themselves to clothing as you brush past. Spirits from the forest could be quite pesky once they'd got it into their head you needed to do something for them. Whole villages often had to move if the spirits decided it was time to play their impish games. Bad luck would manifest in the communities until the entire population was forced to pack up and arrive in the place that the spirits needed them to be.

If his dream was inspired by tree spirits then this would also explain why the wild boar was appearing to him and talking about buffaloes. Spirits were obsessive about buffaloes. Whenever there was bad luck in a village the starting point was always to sacrifice a buffalo to appease the mischievous phantoms of the forest.

Maybe it was the timing. Last time he'd had the dream was the night after Old Papa Han's funeral. This time it was after learning that Mr Salt's wife was suffering from an illness that could be life-threatening if she didn't get the treatment soon. No, maybe the timing was not the key. They were not really the same thing. Perhaps it was just the anxiety, or the fact that his mind was wandering now that his daily routine had been disturbed.

He thought about waking his wife to tell her about the dream. They could see if she could think of any other reasons that he'd had the dream again. She and Mama Tae had actually made a bit of money on the lottery last time they'd punted on his numbers with the additional tree information. If he told her he'd had the dream again then she'd probably rush out and stake their life savings on it. Sharing his most recent recap of the vision might not be such a priority after all.

22. Sleepless

Mr Tann was also having a difficult night. The unexpected appointment of Mr Hua Lin as Branch Manager had been eating away at him for weeks. It was the injustice that really got to him. The lack of respect that had been shown to him by the managers at head office was a disgrace. That job was his by rights. He'd earned it after years of faithful service. No one had even discussed it with him. They just sent that young upshot down to his province who'd never even been a manager before. What did he know about running things in a place like Maklai. Mr Tann had served in the bank for most of his working life. How dare they treat him in this dismissive way?

Equally frustrating was the additional strain that being overlooked for manager had added to his marriage. Or more specifically, the additional strain his marriage was causing him. His wife had always been disappointed with him. Her sister had married into a family with a company that made a lot of money in the building trade. Her husband had been set up with the logistics side of the business and now owned a fleet of about ten lorries. The brother-in-law had been one of the first people in town to by a pick-up truck for the family. Whilst his sister was flouncing around in her big car and sending people running every time she careered down the street, Mr Tann's wife had been relegated to walking each day to the market and back. She complained that it was so humiliating.

The one comfort that Mrs Tann had tried to cling on to all these years was that Old Papa Han had been on the eve of retirement for as long as anyone could remember. Once he'd gone, her husband would be provincial manager of the Khoyleng Bank in Maklai province. The money of course would never match that of her sister's family. However, there would be prestige and the opportunity to network with the powerful in the same way that Papa Han had done. It was this long held hope that had enabled her to hold back her sour glares and cutting remarks. Now that the reality of her husband's failure at the bank had hit, she had no incentive to stop herself from unleashing a whole marriage-worth of frustration and hatred towards the poor man. Mr Tann had begun to dread going home. In the past he had always locked up the bank at 4.30pm on the dot. These days he was getting later and later to reduce his contact time with the embittered old dragon. When he did return he was subjected to a barrage of comparisons between him and his brother-in-law. It was all about the money. How well the sister had done, and how poor Mr Tann was. How he was useless, couldn't get a well-paid job, wasn't respected by society, wasn't respected by the bank. She'd have been better off marrying anyone but him. Dr Gaiek from the hospital, for example. He would have married her, she was sure of it. But no, she'd been foolish enough to marry Tann, and look at where that had got her. Nowhere.

Mr Tann was coming to the end of his tether. Something was going to have to change soon or he would lose it. As he lay awake in the early hours he started to consider whether he could pay someone to help his wife have an 'accident'. No, that wouldn't work. As Mrs Tann regularly pointed out, they didn't have much money. Arranging a hit on someone was said to be quite costly. If he had the kind of money needed to pay for a hit man then his wife wouldn't be torturing him like this in the first place.

Whilst he was going through his insomniac late night scheming, the second choice that occurred to him was to help Mr Hua Lin have an 'accident'. On review, for the time being that plan came up against some very similar constraints to the ones that had led him to rule out doing away with his wife.

Hua Lin was the enemy, of course. He had taken Tann's rightful job away from him. Job theft aside, of late there were other elements of the new manager's activities that had become even more annoying to Mr Tann. The joy of having Papa Han about the place was that the old man was so un-intrusive. He had just sat in his office all day, quietly going over the books of accounting, and rarely interfering with anything that Mr Tann did. This Hua Lin meanwhile had virtually turned the whole place upside down in his determination to shake things up. In spite of this, Hua Lin was no Mr Perfect himself. Lately he had been coming to work at least twice a week with bleary red eyes and his breath stinking of cheap booze. It was no way for a manager of a respected provincial bank to conduct themselves in working hours. If he wanted to change everything at the bank then maybe he should change his own questionable ways as well.

Mr Tann rolled over in bed and stared at the stars beyond the open shutters of his window. He wished he was able to sleep properly. All this scheming just made him feel more awake. Most nights in recent times he just lay awake worrying about things, and that made it all the more difficult to concentrate at work the next day. It was what people called a vicious circle. It was so difficult to concentrate at the bank if you were tired. That was how mistakes were made. If he started making mistakes then he was liable to not only miss out on promotion but lose his current job as well.

As Mr Tann contemplated this rather worrying outcome, a devilish thought crossed his mind. He knew what the consequences would be of him making a mistake at work, however, what were the consequences of Mr Hua Lin making mistakes? Mr Tann was quite sure that he was not the only one to have noticed the alcohol fumes as the new manager passed through the bank. The prim and proper Mrs Yea-bo had rolled her eyes for the benefit of Mr Tann on several occasions from behind her cashier's window as Hua Lin had wafted past. Right now there was easy access at the bank to poorly secured piles of cash. A slightly intoxicated provincial manager would be an easy target to blame if it was found that any of this cash was missing. Particularly as it was the manager's idea to have more cash than the safe could properly hold. Mr Tann could sneak some money for himself, and with any luck get Mr Hua Lin blamed and sacked.

Mr Tann smiled a rare and wry grin. Mr Tann had been at the bank for years and nothing had ever gone missing. No one would look to blame him, but the new manager had been around for only a few weeks and would quickly come under scrutiny. This time Mr Tann would know to make a prompt proactive communication with the bosses in Khoyleng. Show them that in a crisis he was the man to turn to. They'd soon see that they could easily do without the young upstart from the city. What they needed was a mature and responsible man that was respected by the community. The bank would be run just as well if not better with Mr Tann at the helm.

Mr Tann began to doze off with a look of contentment on his face. It was the first real sleep he'd had in weeks.

23. Early

Kheng arrived at his afternoon shift a little earlier than expected. He'd had an unsettled morning, thinking through the implications of his recurring dream, and he wanted to get on with doing something to take his mind off things. It had occurred to him that the dream might be a visitation by disgruntled tree spirits that were upset with him. Often in these cases the only solution was to move house. They might even have to move to a new province. Perhaps the tree at the start of the dream was literally a mischievous tree spirit, doing a kind of opening speech as a formality to start off the rest of the dream. He really hoped that wasn't the case. He was far too old to pick up his life and start afresh.

Meebor was sitting on the chair by the gate, taking the batteries out of the torch and then putting them back in, but in a different order.

"Afternoon, Mr Kheng. That Mrs Khamgenn has been in again this morning. That's three times in the last week that I've seen her. They must be raking it in at that hardware store of theirs. You know, the one that's on the corner opposite the market. I noticed there was a whole load of new water-pump engines out the front of their shop the other day. They must be doing some good trade to have that kind of stock in. Oh well, not much use knowing that now that I've gone straight is there? It's probably a good tip for someone thinking of giving the place the once-over though."

"What if she's putting money in, not taking it out?"

"Wealth is wealth, Mr Kheng. They don't keep it in the bank for long. People still think of savings as their assets. They don't trust the paper that goes inside the bank and turns into numbers on a computer. They'll be buying jewellery, some property, or a new TV or something. It can all be turned back to money quite easily if they decide they need to."

Kheng decided to change the subject. Mostly in case Mrs Khamgenn came back out of the bank while they were still planning to theoretically filch from her all that she had.

"Did you hear about Mr Salt's wife. Salt says that she's in hospital. They took her in yesterday on account of her kidneys apparently. They want to put her on one of those expensive machines. It sounds really quite serious. It could go very badly for his wife if they can't afford to pay for use of the machine."

"Well he's not going be able to cope with that on his guard's salary. Maybe I should put him onto the Mrs Khamgenn idea."

"You've got the torch then, Mr Meebor?"

Kheng had concluded that a rapid handover was the easiest way to get Meebor to move on and avoid an embarrassing incident with Mrs Khamgenn. Meebor signed the handover book and told Kheng that if he came up with any ideas for helping out with Salt's wife, and if there was anything he could do to support, then just to let him know. With that he scooted out of the gate to make the most of the extra time that it appeared Kheng wanted to give him by turning up too early.

Kheng took the old red plastic chair that Meebor had left under the tree, set it down next to the gate and returned to contemplate his dream. It had bothered him all morning, but he'd not really been able to focus on it as his wife had been going on about mending an old set of shelves. They had been under the house where the chickens roosted, but she wanted to use them in the kitchen for keeping plates. Why was he suddenly dreaming about his long since departed Aunt Kaylin, his father's older sister? His main memory of her was the time when they lived in the village and she came to stay with them for several months. She was mean. Mean to his father and mean to him. He couldn't really remember why she had turned up as he'd been quite young at the time. He had an idea that she was on her own, it was possible that she'd been left by her husband, and moved in with them as she had nowhere else to go. She would take out her frustrations at her failure by ordering Kheng to do chores all day. He would be sent to fetch firewood, collect water, get roots from the forest, mill the unhusked rice. The chores were hard work. They made his arms ache and feel like they had fire in them they burned so much with the pain. He'd missed out on quite a lot of school that year. There was also the incident at the market as well. Some of his childhood was a distant memory but that day in the market had remained with him as vividly as if it were yesterday. The thought of the market could always turn a pleasant daydream into a waking nightmare.

Kheng was distracted by his visionary contemplations for the rest of the shift. Even his 4.30pm interaction with Mr Tann, who was still expressing his deep annoyance at the overwhelming amount of cash building up in what used to be a quiet provincial bank, failed to distract him from his deliberations.

It was well after ten that evening when Mr Salt rolled up at the gates, late once again for his shift.

"Mr Kheng. Sorry to be delayed again. I remembered the coffee this time. Brought two cups. I'll just sign in the book for the torch. Then we can have a brew."

The coffee was really more of an excuse to talk again about his wife. Mr Salt sat on the front steps of the bank while Kheng sat on the chair and listened. Kheng felt quite sorry for Mr Salt. He clearly had no one but his wife and their two kids. Without his wife he'd be utterly lost and he had no one else he could talk to. Kheng observed there was a certain tragedy in the knowledge that the man whom Mr Salt had recently met and saw for two minutes a day so they could confirm the presence of a chair and a torch before parting ways was now his closest confident. After Salt had unburdened himself, they just sat there in silence for a while, staring out at the night and listening to the occasional insect or distant bark of a dog.

Having realised Salt wasn't going to let him go until they'd finished a second coffee, Kheng decided it was time to shift his thoughts to other things, and to tell him all about the dream.

Salt listened intently to Kheng's detailed description of his vision before giving his opinion.

"Maybe the problem is that you're looking for just one meaning, Kheng. I mean, with the buffalo, there's clearly a forest spirit involved. Making you have your dream. But what if the buffalo is just there to help realise that this is a forest spirit talking to you? More of a point of reference. Not the message itself. The moon bit seems to be about wealth. Wealth at night I guess. As for your Aunt Kaylin, only you can really work out where she comes in. Was she famous for anything?"

"Not really famous outside of our family. Finding trouble and inflicting pain were her usual achievements from what I remember of her."

"So a bit of a snake then. Maybe you were trying to dream of a snake but she came up by accident. That can happen apparently. My wife used to be into all that dream stuff. She would say that the person you should be dreaming of can appear as an animal or a tree, and then the person you actually dream of is representing something else. It can be all very confusing. Was Aunt Kaylin interested in triangles at all?"

Kheng shook his head. He couldn't quite see where Mr Salt was going with this. 'Connecting the dots' should normally involve dots where a reason to connect had been identified. It was not just connecting dots because they were dots.

"What about the moon? Was it a crescent or was it full?"

"The moon was full, like a big golden circle."

"Well, the moon is just about full now. Totally full tomorrow, I would think. So maybe you're going to come into some wealth. Money left to you by your snaky Aunt Kaylin? Or maybe whoever that tree represents has got something to do with it? Whatever it is, looks like it could happen tomorrow."

Kheng shook his head.

"No hope of that. Aunt Kaylin died penniless years ago. And if she did have any wealth the miserable old woman would have worked out how to take it all with her."

Superficial though Salt's early analysis had been, it had given Kheng something to think about. There was no longer any doubt in his mind that a tree spirit of some sort was behind all of this. Everyone seemed to confirm that the buffalo element was proof beyond doubt. He was also inclined to accept that the vision of the golden moon, just a day before the real moon would be full, was setting the parameters and timing for whatever the dream was foretelling. So, he'd figured out the 'who' in part, and he understood the 'when' but the all-important 'what' still eluded him. Kheng explained all of this to Mr Salt.

"Well, Mr Kheng. You'd better head home and start dreaming again. See if you can get this spirit back. Get him to add a bit of clarity to all of this. At least try not to wake up until after your Aunt Kaylin's done her turn. I'll try and get a good night's sleep too. See if I get anything that might help."

Kheng thought it unlikely that Salt would be able to contribute through an additional dream. After all, Salt had never met his Aunt Kaylin. Besides, it was unlikely either of them was going to get much sleep after all that coffee.

Kheng negotiated the plank-covered trench while Salt went over to the outside tap and washed out the coffee mugs. Kheng then started to make his way home. He had been left with one final niggling thought. Salt had said that trees could appear in dreams but really they might be a person. Somewhere in his mind Kheng felt he should know who that could be, but he just couldn't reach far enough into his sub-conscious and grab the answer.

24. Opportunity

Ms Win-Kham had been following a simple three-stage plan for the entrapment of her new boss, Mr Hua Lin. The stages were fairly straightforward: flatter, ingratiate and ensnare.

Stage one – flattery – had been initiated at their first meeting after the welcome lunch. Since then it had been applied liberally whenever an opportunity presented itself. Stage two – ingratiate – had been put into action shortly after Hua Lin stepped into his new office. For several weeks now Ms Win-Kham had been inveigling her way under the skin of Mr Hua Lin. Each morning she was the first of the bank clerks to arrive, not including the bumbling old Mr Tann of course, who seemed to be getting increasingly erratic with his working hours. She was the first to greet Mr Hua Lin with enthusiasm as he entered the building, enquire sympathetically after him, and then rush to make him a coffee. Throughout the day she would ensure she was on hand to aid him with the slightest of problems. Perhaps there was an error in the ledger, a customer that was lingering too long in his office, a fly annoyingly refusing to accept that the open window it arrived through could have equal utility as a way to get out. Ms Win-Kham was there to correct, usher and swat, as the situation demanded. She was his 'go-to' employee and gradually she believed that she was becoming indispensable to him.

It wasn't all about time and devotion, she was financially investing quite heavily in her ambitions as well. She had bought a number of new outfits for the office. They guaranteed that she was respectable and appropriate, whilst making sure her look was always flattering to her figure and displayed just enough leg to get a regular glance from her employer. Contrary to the other well-to-do women who got their hair and make-up done early on a Friday or Saturday evening so as to be glamorous for the social events of the weekend, Ms Win-Kham had changed her beautifying appointment to early on a Monday morning so that she was at her most glamorous when she presented Mr Hua Lin's morning coffee at the start of each week. Occasionally she would top up the coiffure and artistry on a Wednesday afternoon if she became concerned her resplendence wouldn't make it all the way to Friday. Of course, the other women in the bank noticed this, but it was only spoken of in hushed whispers behind closed doors. To be so indiscreet as to say something directly would only underline their own insecurities rather than unbalance those of Ms Win-Kham. The men in the office were just pleased to have someone attractive in their midst and failed to question a deeper motive.

All of the 'stage two' ingratiating was building a useful foundation for Win-Kham's higher goals, but it wasn't ever going to be a game changer. Ms Win-Kham knew this. If there were cuts at the bank and staff had to go then perhaps she would be a few places further from the top of the list of those to immediately receive the boot. However, it was a national bank, and she was a semi-government employee. Those sorts of jobs were 'jobs for life'. Even if the country ran out of money they would still all go in each day as normal and sit at their empty desks to wait for the government to find some more. Meanwhile, the current level of ingratiation meant that her necessity to Mr Hua Lin was only in his daily work. She was not a necessity in his life. Once he left the office each evening Ms Win-Kham became an irrelevance until coffee was needed the following morning. She needed to consider that one day soon he would find a reason to pack up his provincial career and answer the call to return to the big smoke. Essential though Ms Win-Kham was to Mr Hua Lin in the machinery of the Maklai bank's workings, she was never going to be part of his essential minimal luggage for the onward journey.

It was now that Ms Win-Kham could see an opportunity to put stage three into action: 'ensnare'. If she kept her wits about her, her prey was not far from experiencing what can happen when a woman as determined as Ms Win-Kham initiates the 'ensnare' option.

The bank's security had never been particularly good, but at least the money had always been counted regularly by Mrs Yeo-bo and then put in the safe. Right now, there was money that wasn't in a safe, just a room with a regular lock, and it was as a direct result of a decision from Mr Hua Lin.

Mr Hua Lin was clearly far too trusting and too set on his goal of running the bank with a modicum of regulation. He assumed that the provincial folk were all simple hard working nationalists devoted to the cause. He had failed to look at his rash decision through a more cynical lens. For Ms Win-Kham, it was simple. The money was not locked in the main safe, the extra money that did not fit was being kept in the bank because of Hua Lin. Should some of the money go missing, it would be difficult to prove where it had gone. Other than an unlikely full confession from a perpetrator caught in the act, the fault would lie squarely with the provincial manager. Mr Hua Lin had left himself wide open. The opportunity that he had provided to Ms Win-Kham was so simple it was almost laughable.

If Ms Win-Kham had learned anything in life it was to make sure that when you make a decision you have considered every eventuality. For those eventualities where the decision could backfire, you could identify someone else who looked more responsible than you, and who would take the fall. Clearly Mr Hua Lin had failed to take a similar approach.

Originally, Ms Win-Kham had thought that she would take some of the money from the safe room herself. It would have to be enough money for it to be a problem but not so much that she'd go to prison for most of her life if she was unlucky and caught red-handed in the safe room. However, there was very little chance of that. Once the money was gone from the room it was all relatively simple. The next day she could suggest helping out with a routine cash count. She was one of the more experienced bank staff and it would not seem out of place to say that she was worried about the high quantities of money in the room. Having done the counting, she would then discreetly point out to Mr Hua Lin that some of the cash was missing. He would demand a search and an enquiry. She would then help him to realise that an investigation would look bad. Bad for the bank, but more importantly, devastating for him. The bottom line for head office in Khoyleng was that the money had gone missing on his watch and he had allowed for all that money to be kept outside of the safe. Ms Win-Kham had played out the scene in her mind. The confident and aloof man in the suit with his chiselled facade would become like a young, frightened child with a quivering lip. Once he had calmed down a little Ms Win-Kham would help him to understand how she had the skills to cook the books and cover up the whole thing. He would have no choice but to go along with it. Once they started down the road in a partnership of corruption and secrets, then Mr Hua Lin was well and truly hers, as was his life back in Khoyleng when eventually they both moved there together.

The plan was good, and stage three was all but ready to implement. However, the more that Ms Win-Kham studied the finer details and planned the implementation of her operation, the more she realised it had some minor flaws. She also could see that there was an even easier way to do it, and with much less risk to herself. Firstly she realised that it wasn't as easy as she had thought to gain access to the safe room. It seemed that she was not the only one to have worked out that the new cash levels meant that security was a little compromised. Mrs Yeo-bo was looking increasingly stressed, and not only regularly locked the safe room door each time she used it, but made regular paranoid trips back to the room to check she'd locked it. A plan-B that worked in Mrs Yeo-bo's increasing paranoia might be something to consider but a direct swipe of the money for now was out of the question. There is often innovation in the face of adversity and Ms Win-Kham's lateral thinking soon allowed her to develop a new and deviously elegant scheme.

25. Counting

Mr Tann hadn't achieved very much throughout the day. His job wasn't one that demanded achievement. Ensuring the status quo was a respectable measure of a good job done. However, for much of the day the status quo had been ignored while he sat at his desk and added the details and timing to the ingenious plot that he had concocted the night before. He had meticulously studied the routine of Mrs Yea-bo. He'd studied the routine of Ms Win-Kham. He'd studied the comings and goings of Hua Lin and indeed everyone else in the bank that day. His main interest was the frequency with which people either passed by or entered the safe room. His analysis showed that the key to success in his endeavour was in the lack of money counting that went on throughout the day. He could see that now: he just needed to pick the perfect moment to get into the room where all the cash was.

The bank had never kept overwhelming amounts of cash on site before. Papa Han had known how much they usually got through each week and so would ask the head office in Khoyleng to send down enough money to top them up to a sensible level. The system of counting the cash had not yet adapted to the sudden change of policy whereby far too much money was being stored. There was more cash than there was time to count it unless the roles of several of the clerks were radically revised.

In the old way of doing things, Mrs Yea-bo, the assistant cashier, would count the money as it was delivered. The provincial branch did not have a money-counting machine but the head office in Khoyleng did. Therefore, the money arrived in wads of one hundred machine-counted notes banded together by a thin strip of paper with the bank logo printed on it. Mrs Yeo-bo put 100% trust in the high-tech counting system that had applied the bands of paper, and considered the logo stamped in the middle as if it were an official wax seal. With her unwavering faith she never counted the individual notes, just the number of paper-bound wads, and then she put them all in the safe. This was still how things were done following Mr Hua Lin's change of rules, even though most of the money no longer fitted into the safe but sat on the floor next to it in cloth bags. Mrs Yea-bo counted the number of wads, multiplied by 100, and recorded the result in the ledger as she had always done. This approach had served her well for all her years at the bank and had never caused a problem.

In all his time at the bank, Mr Tann had known that Mrs Yea-bo diligently stuck to this routine. This was the inside knowledge that he would apply to commit his robbery. All he needed to do was find a good reason to be in the money room. The one he was currently favouring was to say that he was looking to see what sort of new safe they might need so that he could propose a 'design' to head office. He'd do a bit of pacing out to measure the space, or maybe even take a tape measure with him and note down the length of the room. Whilst there he would wait for Mrs Yeo-bo to leave and then subtly slip a few notes out of the top of some of the wads and then move them to the back of the piles. It would be a long time before they were used, maybe weeks. Mrs Yea-bo would only be keeping track of the money by counting wads. A wad of 97 notes was pretty indistinguishable from one of a 100 notes unless you counted each one. Yeo-bo's faith in the head office machine guaranteed that she wouldn't. Eventually it would become clear that the bank's ledger was incorrect and that cash was missing from the safe room. However, Mrs Yeo-bo would blame the central bank's counting machine. The management would never accept that, and an investigation would highlight that the new provincial manager had failed to make Mrs Yea-bo count the money properly, keep it in a proper safe and that he was also often a bit intoxicated most mornings when he arrived at work. There was very little question about where the blame would land. Mr Tann would get a bit of extra cash, which after years of service was a small bonus that his conscience could easily justify, and would pave the way to his new promotion at the same time. It was the perfect solution.

26. Cash

Mr Hua Lin dragged himself to his desk after yet another big night out. His head was throbbing. It was painful to try to keep his eyes open and yet he had a full day's work ahead of him. His stomach felt heavy with the volume of beer that he'd endured until the early hours whilst repeatedly toasting the provincial business fraternity.

He'd spent most of his night desperately trying to inveigle his way into the shallow affections of the daughter of Mr Guim. He was the businessman who owned the two big fuel stations that stood like sentries either side of the main town as well as the main one near the old bus station. Mr Guim was an important member of the provincial business community and had a big account at the bank. His fortune was only ever going to get bigger. He had gone to school with the provincial governor and it was that same governor who had granted him one of the very few licences to run a fuel station. More importantly, he had also helped a few people part with their roadside land at more than reasonable prices. His fuel stations could then be built at the most convenient and, therefore, the most lucrative locations in the town. Finally, Guim's friend the governor also controlled who was allowed to tanker fuel into the province in the first place. Guim always got the best deal and his fuel was always a little cheaper than the other fuel sellers. It was a stable monopoly in a visibly competitive sector and a situation which suited Guim and his associates very nicely. Whilst Hua Lin recognised that the business part of Guim's life was enviable, his daughter Lae Souk was turning out to be a total nightmare.

Mr Guim had a very long and manicured thumb nail on his right hand which had been sharpened to a point. On his left hand he'd done something similar with the nail of the little finger which he used to point at text when discussing text in contracts with his business associates. This didn't greatly add to the accuracy of his pointing, but it did regularly bring to everyone's attention that Mr Guim didn't need to work with his hands. He was no peasant slaving in the rice paddies or labourer moving boxes around a warehouse. No, the only time he did need to lift a finger was to point with his pointy nail in a way that reminded others how much power and money he had.

Guim's daughter, Lae Souk, had been brought up so that she could also be displayed like a pointed manicured accessory whose function was to impress on others how much the family was worth. Hua Lin was finding that she had very expensive tastes and very limited conversation. When she did enlighten others with her thoughts, the flow of noise was all about shopping trips for clothes in Khoyleng, and what outfits she needed to buy to match the jewellery her father had given her for her birthday. It was apparently vital for Lae Souk to keep track of what she had worn and when. This was to make sure she didn't die of embarrassment at a society wedding by choosing an ensemble she'd been seen in before, or worse still an outfit that someone else had worn first. These vain priorities were a little lost on Mr Hua Lin. He owned two suits. One of which he wore for work, and the other he kept aside for special occasions. He was of a social background where the diversity of his suit ownership was in itself fairly impressive. Inspirational stories of Hua Lin starting out with nothing and dragging himself from the poor end of town to the streets of success were never going to have a lasting impact on Lae Souk. The hard work and determination of a person climbing the ladder of success wasn't a message to inspire awe. That kind of information meant that you were fundamentally a peasant and you didn't belong anywhere near a set who were born with connections and money. Mr Hua Lin knew that his first task in promoting himself as a potential suitor was to demonstrate his right to move in her social circles. He would never be able to let on that he was perhaps punching above his weight. Wooing Lae Souk wasn't ever going to be an easy challenge. Indeed it was something of a gamble and it seemed highly likely he would become bankrupt before reaching his goal of tying the knot with the family.

Mr Hua Lin sat for a long time behind the closed door of this office, his elbows on the old wooden desk of Papa Han, cradling his aching head in his hands. His plan of marrying into money was not panning out. He could neither face nor afford another night out with the bland and shallow Lae Souk. 'Plan B' was to abandon finding a wealthy marriage and to find a wealthy benefactor instead. The problem was that wealthy benefactors were usually in short supply for someone who started out with nothing from the poor end of town. Desperation, amplified by the pounding in his head, was directing him away from the easier route, and whispering to him that there was also a Plan C.

In the absence of a human benefactor, the remaining

option was going to be an interest-free loan from the room at the back of the bank where all the unsecured money was kept. It would be a loan of course. He would just borrow some. He might even write a note to keep track of the amount to prove his honourable intentions. After all, he was doing this mostly for the good of the bank: the office at Khoyleng should see it as an investment. He would buy himself a marriage with a young woman of influence but more tolerable than Lae Souk Guim and then pay back the cash with the spoils from the wedding gifts. The bank would be none the wiser, Hua Lin would be financially secure plus have his wife's family to back him as he forged ahead with his career. The more he thought about it through the fog of yet another aching hangover, Plan C started to make a lot of sense.

27. Inspiration

It had been a restless night. Kheng dozed and then woke. He dozed a bit more and then woke again, this time in a bit of a panic. He couldn't decide if he'd dreamed the same vision yet again, or if he was just thinking about it so much it was always swimming through his head every time he drifted between sleep and consciousness. Maybe he would be better off going under the house and setting up his hammock between the wooden supports. He never had this kind of trouble sleeping when he was swaying gently, slumbering in the open air of his hammock. He'd always used his hammock when he was with the army, protected from the enemy by the thick canopy above and the scrubby undergrowth that surrounded him. At the bank he'd had content and dreamless sleeps beneath the tree at the back of the bank. Maybe the hammock was where he was supposed to sleep.

That morning Kheng decided to go to the nearby noodle shop for breakfast. There one at the end of the road that made good noodle soup. They didn't skimp on the meat, got the flavours in the soup just right and provided plenty of greens, usually a large chunk of cabbage, long beans, basil and chilli peppers. In spite of his difficult night, he was able to approach the new day with a remarkable amount of clarity. The pieces of the puzzle had now finally come together. It had taken the disjointed suggestions of Mr Salt and a lack of sleep throughout the night to help him to see beyond the jumble of imagery: the tree, the moon, the wild boar, Aunt Kaylin. Of course, the insane rambling of Mama Tae had possibly added a little bit to his thoughts around dream analysis, but looking back she'd caused more confusion than anything else. Anyway, Kheng finally had it all sorted out. There was now no doubt in his mind what the dream had meant and what it meant he had to do about it.

Remarkably, the outcome of all of the interpretation that Kheng had applied to his disturbing vision was rather extreme. The only conclusion that he could reach was that he was destined to rob the Maklai Provincial Bank. If he'd arrived at this staggering revelation a month ago then he would have been utterly shocked. However, having spent so many days being tormented by the dream and its many aspects, it was more of a relief than anything to finally have some understanding, and to know what to do about it all.

Kheng finished slurping the remains of the soup from the bottom of his bowl of spicy noodles. He then drained his glass of thick chewy coffee. He returned home, taking the kind of big confident strides that someone with a renewed purpose in life would use. After a morning of swaying in his hammock beneath his stilt house and adding further details to his analysis, he knew his understanding was sufficient for him to be ready to act. It was with a much lightened heart and greater spring in his step for some time that Kheng made his way to work that afternoon. Meebor, as usual, was hanging around the gates, keeping tabs on the arrival and departure of the more valued customers.

"Afternoon, Mr Kheng. How are you? It's been a busy old morning here. There's no sign of Mrs Khamgenn from the hardware store, but Mr Navey's been in again with a fairly heavy looking bag. If I were looking for a joint in town to turn over, then I think old Navey's jewellery shop is edging its way into the lead. Anyway, I'm ready to head home and get a late lunch. Here's the notebook; sign for the chair and the torch then, Mr Kheng, and I'll be on my way."

A rapid departure from Mr Meebor didn't fit with Kheng's current scheming.

"No, I don't think so, Mr Meebor. This time I think we need to do a proper and organised handover. Check the perimeter, go round the back of the bank to make sure everything is okay, and then do the signing over."

Meebor shrugged.

"If you say so, Mr Kheng. Up to you. But it's all the same as normal back there."

"I do say so, Mr Meebor. Come on."

Kheng gestured, flicking his head to the side to beckon Meebor to follow. As they moved around the side of the bank Kheng peered in through the provincial manager's office. The security computer continued to show its predictable scene: the front gate, the front door and the cashier's desks in the front of the bank.

"Everything okay, Mr Kheng?"

"Yeah, everything's fine. The security cameras are working normally and pointing just where they need to be. It's all good."

Meebor was a little curious about Kheng's sudden concern about the maintenance of the security cameras.

"You're lucky you can see them at all. I noticed earlier when checking through the window that Mr Hua Lin has been sat in front of the screen most of the morning holding his head in his hands. I'm surprised at him. He came across as being so business-like in the interview. All professional and classy, exuding self-confidence. He just looks really tired these days. The pressures of high office must be getting to him. He'd be better off like us, bottom of the food chain, take less pay but let the bosses lose their sleep over all the responsibility. Anyway, why all the sudden concern about the cameras?"

Kheng was thinking about Hua Lin:

"Well, Mr Meebor, if you choose a high responsibility job, and the salary that goes with it, then you have to learn to take the pressure."

Meebor nodded. All this talk of management and responsibility sounded a bit serious when all they needed to do was sign over the torch and the chair. Kheng stood back from the window and thought for a moment. He then proceeded to lead Meebor to the back of the bank. Kheng made his way over to the shade under the jackfruit tree, away from the back door in the far corner of the compound, so they would be out of earshot of any of the clerks using the kitchen area at the rear of the building. Then he turned to face Mr Meebor. His expression displayed a level of seriousness that Meebor had previously never seen in him.

"I need you to come back here, tonight, Meebor. You need to get here shortly after the start of Mr Salt's shift at about quarter past ten. And I need you to do exactly what I say, and when I say it. Can you do that, Meebor? It's important."

"What are you talking about, Mr Kheng?"

"I have a plan that might just solve the impossible problem that Mr Salt has. His wife is desperately in need of treatment, but there's no money. She may die if we don't help. So I have a plan, but I need you here, and we have to do it tonight. It's the full moon tonight, right. I checked with the monks on the way over here and they confirmed it for me. It's definitely the full moon, so this is the only chance we have. It's one in, all in. I saw it all in the dream. If you're not prepared to help then you need to say now."

"What dream?"

"A dream I had. More of a vision really. Like a message from the forest spirits. You don't have to worry about that now, I'll explain it all later. Let's just say that the skills you developed in your shady and regrettable past may be just about to pay off."

"What are you talking about, Kheng?"

"Mr Meebor. Tonight, you, me and Mr Salt are going to rob the bank!"

"Rob the bank!?"

"Shushhh. Meebor. Yes. Rob the bank. Well, some of it. But don't worry about the details. This is what I want you to do…"

28. Self-Service

It was about 4.15pm as Mr Hua Lin made his way down the corridor in the bank and spotted the safe room door was ajar. The opportunity was too great to miss and so he pushed the door open and entered. To his surprise, Mr Tann was inside the room reaching for the door handle so he could make his way out. Both gentlemen seemed equally flustered by the crossing of their paths. Mr Tann was the first to offer a reason for his unexpected presence:

"I was just checking dimensions, Mr Hua Lin."

"Hmmm, good. Of what?"

"The room, Mr Hua Lin. Seeing what might fit. What we would be able to get through the door. That sort of thing."

"Right?"

"The safe, Mr Hua Lin. I'm wondering if the door to the room is too small to get a bigger safe inside. We may have to take the window out and hoist it in that way. Or maybe knock down an inner wall then bring it in through the front doors."

Hua Lin stared at Mr Tann with a puzzled expression. It was a long and vacant stare as Hua Lin was far too tired to change his expression back again. Mr Tann panicked a little and gabbled a further explanation.

"For the new safe that we need in the bank, so we can lock up all this extra money. To make sure we follow the Khoyleng regulations and procedures."

"And what did you calculate?"

Hua Lin motioned at Mr Tann's bulging satchel, having leaped to the assumption that, as Mr Tann wasn't clutching a set of drawings and measurements, then they must be stored in his bag.

"What?"

"What did you work out? How big a space do we need?"

"Just thinking through the options for now…pacing things out."

Sweat began to bead on Mr Tann's brow as he clung on to the battered old satchel even tighter for fear Mr Hua Lin might make a grab for it.

Hua Lin was sweating a bit as well. He'd been blaming the previous night's alcohol intake for his leaky skin, but if Mr Tann was perspiring as well then perhaps it really was too hot in the safe room.

"Well, maybe we should meet tomorrow and you can discuss your ideas, Mr Tann."

"That would be great. I'll look forward to it."

Mr Tann scuttled off with a sense of relief and headed for his desk. Mr Hua Lin quickly grabbed a couple of wads of bank notes and stuffed them into his jacket pockets. He then closed the door behind him and followed Mr Tann back down the corridor, cursing his luck. As he passed Mr Tann's room he stuck his head round the corner of the door:

"Shall we say 11.00am?"

"Huh?"

"11.00am. Tomorrow. To discuss the calculations for the safe?"

"What? Yes. Eleven. Let's do that at eleven then. Okay?"

Hua Lin closed Mr Tann's door and returned to his office. It was almost laughable that he had taken the extra step to shore up his alibi by following Mr Tann into, and then immediately out of, the safe room. What cash he'd taken wasn't even enough to fund a weekend with the impossibly vain and extravagant Ms Lae Souk should he bother to pursue that line. It was scarcely enough to get him through the upcoming evening of karaoke that he had planned with Mr Liangtok and his associates. Although, at least there was a chance that Liangtok's daughter couldn't be any more horrendous than Lae Souk. Now, despite his upcoming social expenses and continuing run of poor luck, he would have to meet Mr Tann in the morning for a tedious conversation about something he hadn't even wanted the old dinosaur involved in. Hua Lin would have to come up with a new way to lift from the safe room the considerable sums that he needed to fuel his expensive lifestyle and keep up with the wealthy provincial socialites. He couldn't risk a second encounter with other staff while he did it.

29. Elegance

Ms Win-Kham left the bank that afternoon with a smug, albeit wry, grin spreading across her face. Operation 'ensnare', the final part of her three-phase strategy, was in play. It was while she had been watching Mrs Yeo-bo manically check that she'd definitely locked the door to the safe room for the umpteenth time that Ms Win-Kham realised the weakness of her original plan. The only people who had keys to the safe room were Mrs Yeo-bo and old Mr Tann. Therefore they were the only people who could really get away with taking the money: anyone else planning to do so would need to enlist a key-holder as an accomplice. An accomplice wasn't really an option for operation 'ensnare'. Ms Win-Kham really needed to win this one on her own.

Having seen her error, Ms Win-Kham had almost given up. She was not a bad person or someone who enjoyed having to manipulate and deceive in order to get her own way. However, she was a woman with limited prospects in a male dominated sector. Indeed, it was a male dominated culture: it was her situation that was forcing her to play the hand that she had been dealt.

As Ms Win-Kham hesitated, ruing the efficiency of Mrs Yeo-bo's door-locking paranoia which was preventing

Win-Kham from hatching her devilish scheme, she realised that her plan, with a slight tweak, would still work very nicely without the safe room money. The aim of operation 'ensnare' was to make certain that Mr Hua Lin was sufficiently indebted to her, albeit in a slightly illegal way, to give her the leverage to control him. The original plan was to steal some money and convince Hua Lin that it was his fault the money was gone. She would then cook the books to rescue him from certain arrest and achieve his eternal gratitude and loyalty. The new Plan B was far simpler, but would be equally effective.

Ms Win-Kham realised that all she had to do was cook the books in the first place. Most people involved in book cooking are doing so, as with Plan A, to hide the fact that they've taken money that they shouldn't have, and therefore, when reviewing the books for error, these are the first people look for. In theory, the book cooker will have subtly increased the outgoings so that the documents show more money used and therefore the remaining amount of cash is lower than expected: then they pocket the difference.

This is a classic ploy for people whose aim is to steal money. Ms Win-Kham's revelation was that she didn't need to steal money, just put Hua Lin in a situation where he believed that he was responsible for some that had been stolen. That could be done without actually physically committing the crime itself. She would cook the books to make it look like the remaining cash in the safe room was not enough in comparison with the ledgers. She would then quietly show this 'evidence' to Hua Lin, demonstrating that there was less money than there should be. Having created sufficient panic and desperation she would then console the poor man by reminding him that only she had figured this out. No one else knew. She would then guide him to conclude that together as partners they could scheme their way to a solution. In doing this, she would guarantee that the only available solution was for Ms Win-Kham to cook the books to save her boss's career. He would then be in debt to her for the rest of his life. Once the cooking scheme was agreed by Hua Lin, all Ms Win-Kham had to do was return to the ledgers and put everything back to how it should be. The books would be correct, the money in the safe would have never changed, and no crime would have ever been committed. Meanwhile her prey, Mr Hua Lin, would be well and truly 'ensnared'.

Tomorrow, Ms Win-Kham planned that she would show Mr Hua Lin her tampered version of the books. She would then insist that she alone carry out a full cash count in the safe room. Of course, she would not tell Mrs Yeo-bo why she was doing this. She'd probably tell her that Mr Hua Lin had ordered it as part of the stricter adherence to the regulations. That would be perfectly plausible especially considering all the recent changes at the bank following his arrival. She would then return to the distraught Mr Hua Lin and use her skills and charm to make everything all right. With any luck this would be further inspiration for Mr Hua Lin to leave the Maklai backwaters and take himself, and the woman he believed to be his guardian angel, back to the high society of Khoyleng city.

Ms Win-Kham made her way home. She crossed the road opposite the old market and made her way down the dusty side street that led to her small house. She delicately pushed the gate forward so as not to further challenge its one remaining rusty hinge. As she did so, she took a moment to look at the small and uninviting building that was currently her home. The landlord had not painted it since it was built more than thirty years earlier. Even when the building was newly built it would have been a fairly undesirable residence. Some of the outer walls were now crumbling: clearly there had been insufficient cement in the blocks when they had been made. Creeping plants and weeds were starting to get into the gaps and make things worse. The landlord didn't care. He'd get the same rent with or without repairing it. So why bother to make the repairs? What if the landlord didn't care, what difference did it make any more? Win-Kham decided that right now she didn't care either. She gave the sad little building one more hard look, knowing that her days of living in this disgraceful excuse for a home were almost over. She walked up to the kitchen door and let herself inside so she could start cooking the rice. Her next house would be hers, and she was going to care about it more than anything else in the world.

30. Action

Mr Salt arrived about twenty minutes late for the nightshift. His coffee mugs were out of his bag almost before he'd made it through the gates.

"Mr Kheng. How goes it? Not so well at my end. Sorry to be late. They're still keeping my wife in. No real improvement yet. Not getting worse either. Such a worry. I had to sell some of our stuff today down at the market. If you need any furniture or anything let me know. I'll have to start thinking about selling the house next. Couldn't even give my daughter money for lunch at school today. I've never sold a house before. Only bought the one after we married. I guess it's more difficult these days. Need lots of documents. More costs before you can get the money."

Kheng nodded, and took the flask from him.

"Come on, let's sit round the back of the bank under the hammock tree and talk. Mr Meebor should be here soon as well."

Sure enough, almost as soon as they poured the coffee, there was the faint rustle of leaves crunching under foot and Mr Meebor appeared at the far side of the building.

"Good that you're here, Mr Meebor. Did you come over the wall like we discussed?"

"Yes, Mr Kheng."

"And you came across the front through the tunnel? Nobody saw you?"

"Yes, yes. It wasn't easy though. It took me about five minutes to get my old man's hunting rifle back out through the drain's inspection hatch. It's a difficult angle you see and the rifle has a really long barrel."

"What?!"

"The angle. It was difficult. For the rifle barrel. Not such a problem on the way in though. Not sure why that was. Maybe it's to do with the angle that I was crouching at inside the drain, 'cos I got it in through the top from the outside okay."

"No. I mean 'what' are you doing bringing a hunting rifle to the bank? And where did you get that museum piece?"

"This? It's the old man's hunting rifle like I said, from when he was in the village. Seen a few good stories, has this. And provided the bush meat for some famous feasts that have become woven into the tales of the village history. My gun was taken by the authorities last time I was caught for robbery and sent away. Arguably, I suppose it wasn't really my gun anyway. Either way, at short notice I don't have access to a pistol, just this thing. But technicalities aside, this is a robbery, right? Of a bank? Normally you have to be fairly tooled up to do these things or there's no incentive for anyone to let you in and help you to help yourself to all the money. Hence the firearm, Mr Kheng."

"We are the guards, Mr Meebor. We're the ones that theoretically you need to point that ridiculous thing at so that you can be let in. Besides, it's nearly as tall as you are. If this was a conventional daylight robbery then the front of it would be in the bank a good few seconds before the rest of you. What are you going to do? Provide an accurate but mild injury to the bank teller and then ask everyone else to wait for a bit while you reload with shot and pour the black powder in? This isn't a wild boar hunt. Besides, this is a clandestine night time operation in an empty bank with inside collaborators – namely us. Silence is the key. What if that antique goes off accidentally? Put the thing down somewhere out of sight. We definitely will not be needing it for this job."

Meebor shrugged. In his experience robbing somewhere important like a bank was better done armed. No matter what method you were going for. If something went wrong and you needed an edge, then the gun was the edge of choice. He should be thanked for this thorough preparation for all consequences, not berated the moment he snuck over the wall. However, to avoid a confrontation early on in the caper, he walked over to a shadowy corner of the compound and propped the aging rifle against an old tree stump.

"Good. Now that the weaponry issue is sorted out we can start. Both of you wait here, and I'll go and do the same as Meebor. I'll leave the bank normally so the cameras see me, and then sneak back in over the wall and past the cameras so there's no record that I stayed. The film on the security computer will show that it's business as usual."

With that Kheng picked up his rucksack, and left the compound through the gate.

Mr Salt sat in the hammock, nursing his coffee and looking bemused:

"What is he talking about, Mr Meebor? Why did you bring your father's rifle. Actually, why are you here?"

"Probably best to wait for Kheng to return. He can tell you better than I can."

A few minutes later Kheng had returned, having walked a little way down the road and then doubled back.

He'd climbed into the storm drain system at the front of the bank and crawled his way the short distance past the front entrance, up through the space where the inspection cover was due to be built. After that he'd got back over the wall.

Kheng picked up the mug that he'd left on the ground near to the jackfruit tree. He caught his breath, and took a long gulp of the warm coffee. He then began to provide his two colleagues with an explanation of the night's agenda.

"It seems to me that the three of us all have different problems that are interlinked. Linked to each other and linked to the bank. First is Mr Meebor. During every moment that he stands guard in business hours he is mentally lining up all of the bank's customers as potential targets for burglary. It's only a matter of time before he weakens and gives in to temptation. He'll either be arrested, viciously assaulted by his wife, or probably both."

Meebor grinned and nodded in acknowledgement. Kheng had him sussed out all right. He'd even taken a long route home that afternoon, past Mr Navey's house, just to have a look and do some recreational joint-casing. It was in his blood, and acting on his instincts would someday be inevitable. He couldn't deny a bit of an intervention right now from Kheng was fairly well timed, although rather unlikely to have any significant impact.

Kheng continued:

"Meanwhile, Mr Salt is about to sell his home and take his children out of school so that he can get the vital hospital treatment needed for his wife. Even that extreme measure is only a stopgap. It's only going to put the problem off for a few weeks. The long-term solution needs long-term money. This is by far the most serious of the three problems. He has no family support and no savings.

Meebor, you and I are part of his team. We help each other out. Right now we are the only option for help that Mr Salt has."

Meebor raised an eyebrow but remained silent. He wasn't totally sold on the unshakeable team spirit thing. After all, they'd only known each other for much less than a month. However, he decided that he'd wait and see where Mr Kheng was going with all of this.

"Finally, I am being tormented by a meddling forest spirit which is regularly inveigling its way into my dreams each night and causing me to obsess about the full moon, a talking wild boar and my currently-deceased Aunt Kaylin. It seems to understand my life from childhood until now, and I may never sleep peacefully again until I appease the pesky little troublemaker. Three people, three problems, one solution. That's why the three of us have to rob this bank. What's more, we have to do it tonight."

31. Explanation

Kheng's two colleagues looked back at him with desperately perplexed expressions, indicating that further explanation would be useful.

"It's all in the dream, you see."

The expressions before him failed to morph into something less glazed or bemused.

"The dream is telling me I have to steal. The triangle is us. The three sides of the buffalo's plan. The full moon is the money. And also it's just the moon. Tonight's full moon in fact."

Mr Salt smiled:

"You've finally worked it out then, Mr Kheng. I knew you'd get there in the end."

"Yes. The key to this entire puzzle was the tree. It was there all along but I just didn't see it. You remember you said that sometimes trees can be people and people can be trees, in dreams anyway. Well last night I remembered being at Old Papa Han's funeral. As I had watched the flames rise in the pyre and consume his coffin, I had imagined that he would be reincarnated as a mighty tree, deep in the forest. It was that same night that I first had the dream. The tree in the dream was Old Papa Han. Somehow he knew that I believed that he'd passed to the next life as a mighty tree and appeared before me in that form, right at the start of the vision. This is Old Papa Han helping us out. He was telling me that the three of us have to take some money from his bank to solve the problems: in the dream the wealth comes to us from a full moon. Tonight is the first full moon since the dreams began, so it has to be done now."

Meebor still looked perplexed:

"What dream?!"

"Oh, right. You don't know do you?"

Kheng had quite overlooked that fact that he'd not been involving Meebor in his recent dream analysis. He quickly explained the whole thing in detail to Meebor so that he was fully up to speed. Meebor gave it all some deliberate thought before eventually adding to the analysis:

"So this pig then? What was that about?"

"Yes, I've been thinking about that. My wife snores quite loudly so for a while I suspected the wild boar was a bit of transmission interference. I figured that if I'd been in the hammock at the back of the bank then maybe a colourful bird or a butterfly might have been the bearer of the message. However, then I realised the first dream did happen when I was at the bank, and it was still the wild boar that spoke. Either way the animal was the forest spirit taking the form of a creature so that it could speak the message. Unless of course the pig has any special significant to either of you two. After all, you are part of the triangle it spoke of."

"Right. Plants can't speak and don't have a mouth. I get that, but why use a pig not a person? Why is a speaking pig more acceptable than the spirit deciding to look like and then speak like a person? Why doesn't Papa Han just appear in person and lay out the whole scheme in front of you?"

"I don't know. 'Cos that's not how dreams work. It's probably not how tree spirits work either. When did you last wake up from a dream where someone you know had given you a full set of clear and memorable instructions and then you got out of bed, decided it all sounded very sensible, and then followed them to the letter?"

Meebor considered this explanation for a moment before replying.

"Okay. So, one more question then. If we are to rob the bank, how do you plan to do it?"

"Well, getting in is the easy part. We just go in through the back door."

Kheng looked as their faces returned to expressions of puzzlement, and sensed further details would be necessary.

"Well, you see, the reason for choosing the back door as our way in is that I already have a spare key."

32. Locks and Hinges

Security measures on a building are rarely foolproof. Most are primarily put in place to slow down a potential miscreant, or to deter them from bothering to break in in the first place. Logic would tell them that it would be less effort to break into somewhere else less secure. However, there is usually a way to get around most security measures if you have the time and inclination. This was very much Kheng's opinion anyway. A good example from recent times was the video camera aimed at the front gate at the bank. It was marginally inconvenient; however, given some motivation and an absence of any other priorities, this security obstacle was easily overcome. Kheng now always made the choice to climb over the wall in the corner of the compound when he wanted to pop out during the evening shift to go home for his dinner.

The back door of the bank was another security measure that Kheng had felt inclined to master. The building where he worked was not purpose-built as a bank, it was just a regular place on the main street modified for the purpose many years ago. Despite its formal and business-like veneer at the front, at the back it was very much like every other building in the street. There was a large wooden door which would originally have opened into a small family kitchen area. Now the room was a place where the bank staff with indoor jobs could take their coffee breaks and eat their lunch if they didn't want to go down the road to the noodle shop. More importantly, it led into the bathroom where the toilet was. Kheng had never been a jealous person and by and large accepted his lot and position in life. However, the unkempt and rather alfresco latrine in the back corner of the compound that he was expected to use was smelly, fly-ridden, had gaps at the bottom of the walls where the wooden boards had rotted away, and had never been emptied. In the face of this, Kheng had felt a little neglected compared with the other staff. The prim and well-dressed office staff were rewarded with a tiled and hygienic modern convenience for their needs, meanwhile Kheng was locked out at night with the run-down rat infested health hazard as his only choice. Being a man of gathering age, it was unavoidable that he would need to negotiate the rodent-filled facility several times throughout the night, and he was rather irked at the injustice of his options.

Meanwhile, security, as Kheng had often pontificated, was only there to slow you down. It was never impregnable. Also, for many years Kheng had had quite a lot of time each night in total solitude at the bank, more than twelve hours a day in fact, so being slow was no particular constraint.

Kheng's opportunity came shortly after his first year at the Maklai provincial branch. Mr Tann informed Kheng in their regular evening exchange of grumbling farewells that he was planning to be away for three days to go to his village and attend the funeral of an uncle. It wasn't a particularly well-loved uncle or one he held in any kind of high esteem. However, there was an expectation from the family that he would have to shuffle all the way out there and watch his brothers get drunk and unruly. What could he do? He would get no enjoyment from this enforced leave. Kheng immediately rallied in a show of support and offered to take charge of locking the bank's doors each evening for him. Mr Tann had declined the offer. It saddened him to do so as Kheng would no doubt be very committed to the task. However, the old boy Papa Han would have to do the job himself for a change, as really the bank was his responsibility. Mr Tann did accept, however, that Papa Han would probably struggle to get the doors locked with his failing eyesight and shaky arthritic hands. The key for the back door was becoming a bit stiff in the lock so needed some oiling as well. Mr Tann had often mentioned the need for oil but no one who had been subjected to his moaning had developed sufficient verve for the task to help him out. Kheng sympathised with Mr Tann's predicament and agreed to come to work early the next day, and bring some oil from his home to sort it out. Not only would he supervise Papa Han to lock the doors, but he would clean up the keys and oil the locks as well.

As the bank had been closing up, Kheng had arrived with his usual grubby rucksack swinging from his shoulder and was directed towards the back of the bank and into the kitchen area to wait for Papa Han. Whilst waiting for the old man to make his befuddled way to the rear of the building, Kheng produced a small can of oil, some rags, and some metal polish and began the task of cleaning up the lock, and the door knob, and oiling the mechanism. As he did so Papa Han arrived, producing the large ring that was filled with the bank's many keys, which were jangling together as they were grasped in his shaking hand."

Kheng had been his usual helpful and friendly self:

"Hello, Boss. I'm just oiling the lock like Mr Tann requested. Have you got the key there? I'll give that a bit of a clean as well while I'm here before I lock up."

Papa Han passed over the whole bunch.

"Here Kheng, you work out which is the right key, I can't tell one of the damn things from another."

Kheng took the keys and turned his back on Papa Han. He proceeded to make a lot of noise as he appeared to be attempting to try various keys to find the right one. Had Papa Han not only been able to hear but also see what Kheng was doing he would have known that Kheng had found the right key almost immediately. What he was actually doing was taking the back-door key from the key ring, and replacing it with a different one. Having done this, he turned to Papa Han to make a show of locking the door and testing it to make sure it couldn't open. He then put on a big show of polishing up the key so that it looked good as new and would work much better. He then handed back the bunch of keys to their custodian.

"Mr Kheng you are a marvel. It looks good as new, even with my old eyes."

"Just trying to help, Mr Han."

"Well we'd better get out of here or my wife will be wondering if I've had another one of my black-outs and fallen down somewhere."

Papa Han shuffled off towards the front of the building, and Kheng followed to support with door locking at the front of the building.

As usual, Kheng milled about a bit, inspected the progress of various shrubs by the front wall, swept up a bit of rubbish that had accumulated next to the gate, and then once it was dark he slipped through the gate, as these were in the days long before there were security cameras, and headed home for his dinner. He had decided it was best not to deviate from the normal routine and to avoid arousing any unnecessary suspicion.

When Kheng returned an hour or so later, his rucksack was a little heavier than usual, with a variety of tools and equipment inside, weighing down on top of his trusted hammock. He headed for the back of the bank. He then produced from his pocket the original key for the lock that he had swiped earlier. He turned it gently in the well-oiled lock and the door swung forward.

During the day, Kheng had been to the hardware store on the main road junction near the petrol station and bought an identical locking mechanism for the bank's back door. It included the door knob for each side of the door and the mechanical working for inside. He carefully dismantled the existing locking mechanism in the back door, and then installed the new locking mechanism, but using the original door knobs. Only the inner workings had been replaced. The door would look the same, other than the shiny new key that was now safely tucked unassumingly amongst the many baffling keys that Mr Tann kept on the ring in case one day someone worked out what they might open. Kheng added the two spare keys to his own but less embellished key ring, which until that point had held just the key for his front door.

By the time he'd completed his mission, it was still only 11.30pm. Kheng had expected the delicate operation to take all night, but in the end it had turned out to be quite an easy undertaking. He decided that he'd mark the achievement by going inside and using the facilities.

For the past six years, whenever Kheng had felt a call of nature he'd let himself into the bank. He had not previously shared this hygienic innovation with Salt and Meebor. It was something that required a degree of discipline. He had to make sure there were no muddy footprints left behind in the rainy season, no allowing of curiosity to persuade him to venture beyond the back room and check out the bank, and no forgetting to lock up everything again, exactly as he had found it. One minor slip and the entire scam could be uncovered. He also felt that there was a need to develop a certain level of trust before letting co-workers know that you had changed the locks on the door of a bank so you could let yourself in at night. Having achieved quite a lot of background information on Meebor and Salt in the first few days, Kheng had felt even more justified in the decision to keep his keys to himself. Being the one responsible for lending a key for the back door of the bank to two high profile criminals would not have helped him sleep easy in his bed at night. However, things were different now. The wild boar had spoken of the buffalo and the triangle, and the forest spirits were clearly not going to let up until he appeased them.

33. Ritual

Kheng finished explaining to Meebor and Salt how he'd come by the key for the back door. He then held out his coffee cup to allow Mr Salt to provide a refill. Meebor was the first to respond:

"It's an amazing story, Kheng. You'd have made a great burglar. We could have done with a man like you back in the day. We were always stronger on self-confidence and daring than we were on the technical side of plotting and scheming. Discipline is always a good trait in a burglar."

"Well, I've made sure I looked after the locking mechanism ever since. Oiled it regularly, made sure the fittings are tight. That way they never think about wanting to change the locks again."

Salt made 'hmm' noises to further support Meebor's observation:

"Well, Mr Kheng, I suggest you open up the kitchen door. I can fetch out the large mat. The one that's just next to the sink. You know, the large plastic woven one. They use it when the bank staff want to sit on the floor and share lunch. I can bring it out here. We can perform some convocations before we get stuck into the main part of the robbery."

Kheng turned to Salt with an expression of bemusement:

"Are you sure, Mr Salt? Is it really necessary?"

Kheng had been rather taken aback by this unexpected suggestion. You can never always predict what people's priorities are going to be in a new situation. However, Meebor was quick to comment on the deviation to the plan:

"Unbelievable! First a ban on armaments, and now we're having an opening ceremony. This is the daftest bank robbery I've ever heard of."

"Well, maybe it's important to Mr Salt. He is, after all, dealing with a lot of stress at the moment. And we are basing a lot of this on the slightly obscure advice of a wayward tree spirit. Making sure the spirit in question is still backing the plan might not be a bad move. At least perhaps it will help ease Mr Salt's mind before we get going."

Meebor shook his head. This was nothing like robbing in the old days. People were careful how they chose who to work with. If you were planning a serious heist you'd make sure you never ended up with a crew like this one. He was starting to wonder what he'd got himself into.

Kheng led Meebor and Salt over to the back of the building where he took his keys from his pocket and unlocked the back door. Salt took off his shoes and slipped inside. Soon he was back with the large plastic floor mat. He unrolled it and laid it out on the ground at the back of the bank, putting a stone on each corner to stop it from curling up again.

Mr Salt walked over to where his bag was hanging from a half sawn branch on the trunk of the jackfruit tree. He rooted around in the depths of the main compartment until he found a thin orange candle. He returned, having found a slightly larger flat rock *en route*, and placed it in the middle of the mat. The candle was lit and Salt held it at an angle to dribble hot wax on to the stone until there was enough warm wax in which to place the base of the candle and secure it. With the gathering breeze, the candle burned and flickered furiously.

"Take a seat then Mr Meebor, Mr Kheng."

The three sat down on the mat, facing the candle.

Meebor mumbled as they did so:

"Well we are sitting in a triangle. But there is such a thing as a self-fulfilling prophecy you know."

Mr Salt ignored him and decided to launch into the proceedings:

"Now, has anyone got any gold on them? A ring, pendant, something like that."

Kheng and Meebor gazed at the shadowy face of Mr Salt, as the deep-set cavities of his eyes and length of his nose seemed to expand and contract with the flickering of the flame.

"Not that I know of, why do you ask?" replied Kheng. His tone had become less amicable and more cautious: he felt they were rapidly drifting from his efficiently planned operation.

"If you take an oath and you're wearing gold, then magical spirits looking for mischief can make use of the gold and cause deception. It's a very well-known problem."

Meebor shuffled about on the mat:

"Well, I've got gold in one of my teeth, that one at the back, look."

Meebor leaned over the candle. It was still flickering and the wind-blown wax from beneath the flame was forming an elaborate series of trails down to the stone to create a stalagmite of wax below. He stuck his finger in his mouth, and was pulling his cheek to the side in an attempt to waylay any doubts of his sincerity on the matter.

Kheng was intrigued:

"Where did you get that done? Not in this province I'm sure?"

"No, not in Maklai. It was up in Khoyleng when I was a younger man. One of the times when I was up on my luck I headed to the capital and got it fixed. Dentists weren't what they are today though. None of this hi-tech nonsense. My doctor had one of those drills that you had to power with a foot pedal like an old sewing machine. No pain-killers either. It was worth it in the end though. You wouldn't believe the change it brought. The things I could eat again without the pain."

"It doesn't matter how he got it. We just need to know that it's there."

Mr Salt paused from his outburst while he thought of a solution:

"You'll just have to lean backward. Make it so that your head is outside of the mat. That should be enough to make the risk minimal."

Mr Meebor looked at Mr Kheng. Mr Kheng looked back at Meebor and shrugged. Meebor turned back towards Mr Salt and then shuffled away from him until he reached the edge of the mat before leaning backwards and resting on his elbows. On completion, Meebor turned and raised his eyebrows at Salt to indicate he was now compliant with the instruction, although not necessarily buying in to the reasoning. Mr Salt continued:

"Now then, Mr Kheng, as this is your scheme, you should say the oath."

"The oath, Mr Salt?"

Kheng had not prepared an oath. Neither the designing of oaths, nor the public speaking of oaths, were usually his thing. As far as he was concerned, ceremonial words were the domain of the monks. Much of his younger life, indeed much of his life, had been with the army, he'd never spent time living as a monk. However, in the hope that it would help to move proceedings along, he took a deep breath. The air smelled of the soil, like it did in the rainy season before a shower, and the scent of the damp ground travels on the winds that gambol just ahead of the cloud before the downpour. Kheng took this earthy and pleasing taste in the air as a sign that the spirits were glad that their ethereal wishes were being pre-empted with an oath. He cleared his throat and began:

"I swear, that I have initiated this robbery in good faith, based on the visitation of the spirits of the forest to my dreams, and thorough interpretations there off…"

Kheng looked at the others to see if they were with him on this, or if he was losing the essence of it all, due to his lack of practice. Salt was looking pleased with how things were progressing. Meebor was leaning right back and gazing up at the blackened sky, keeping his molars out of the way of mischievous sprites, so it was difficult to tell. Kheng continued:

"So by taking this oath, we all agree to be respectful of each other and look out for each other, no matter what happens."

"Great," said Salt, grinning widely, "I swear."

"I swear as well," said Meebor in an apathetic tone of voice before allowing himself to sit forwards again. "Can we get on with this robbery now?"

"I think we should," agreed Kheng.

"Do we also need to pray for good fortune and health, like the monks do in Sanskrit?" asked Salt. Clearly, his enthusiasm for ceremony was distracting him a little.

"I don't speak 'monk' and I doubt if you two do either," said Meebor. He had already started to stand up and put his hands behind his back to have a bit of a stretch. "We'd be better off thinking about more practical things, like escape routes and trying not to leave fingerprints."

"Meebor's right," said Kheng. "I think the current oath will have to do. We really need to get on with this now. There's only so much time in one night available for undertaking a bank heist."

As if Meebor's raised voice was the source of the tempest, a gust of wind blew out the candle whilst the first fat drops of rain from the gathering downpour began to rhythmically tap on the plastic mat. Salt grabbed the candle, Kheng took the mat, rolling it as he ran, and not stopping until they were all sheltering under the eaves of the roof by the back door. Despite their haste, by the time they got to the building the drops had rapidly evolved to a heavy downpour and all three of them were drenched.

"Don't anyone go inside."

Kheng's order was dutifully obeyed. He didn't raise his voice very often, but when he did he could sound as commanding as any drill sergeant or captain that he had served under in his army days.

"We can't risk going in the bank and dripping water or mud and leaving any evidence that we were there. We'll have to strip off out here, down to our underwear, leave our clothes by the back door and then go in, wiping our feet on our trousers as we do so."

There was a moment's hesitation before the two guards obeyed their captain and began to remove their outer clothing.

"The rain should be seen as a sign of luck. Like with the harvest. It's if the spirits are with us."

Salt's offering was said to appease the frustration that he had heard in Kheng's voice. Kheng snorted. The rains bringing luck for the annual rice harvest was not his immediate concern.

Once they were inside the kitchen door, Kheng took the

torch and examined the floor for any traces of water from their feet. Superficially, it all looked okay. Things were back on track. Well, in a way. He turned to address Meebor:

"Just before it rained, you raised the issue of fingerprints. What's your view on that?"

"Not good if our prints are found all over the safe room. It's probably best to cover our hands up. Gloves would be the way to go."

"Do you have gloves?"

"No, not really."

Mr Salt reached for his canvas bag.

"I've got some plastic bags. Used them to put the coffee cups in. And spoons and things. There should be enough. We can use them for our hands."

"Okay," replied Kheng. "So pass them out and we can put those on our hands and get moving."

Having mittened-up with the thin plastic bags, the three oath-bound underwear-clad conspirators cautiously made their way through the dark, imposing recesses of the Maklai Provincial Bank.

Part 2

34. The Safe Room

The three men stood in silence, staring at each other, wondering what to do. It had never occurred to any one of them that there would be such an irreconcilable clash of ideologies. Meebor was unwavering in his conviction that a robbery was a get-rich scheme where you took all you could get. The risk involved and the potential consequences didn't diminish much if you decided to be kind to your victim and leave half of it behind. Kheng, meanwhile, was equally confident that they were in the safe room right now on account of his dream and his tree spirit. If not for him, Meebor would be out misguidedly casing Mr Navey's house and Salt would be lying in his hammock fretting about his wife. The higher power from the spirit world was the driving force behind the decision-making, not the petty aspirations of the individuals that were taking part. Finally, Salt was in the bank as a means to an end, the robbery was just a step towards the solution of helping his wife. It wasn't the end game itself. It wasn't a reason to throw away the life he was trying to lead in Maklai.

Eventually Kheng spoke:

"Well, Mr Meebor, I for one am not going on the run from the authorities for masterminding a multi-million nham bank heist and creating the biggest scandal in the history of Maklai, and possible in Feiquon as well. We're here to get the extra that Mr Salt needs to pay for his wife in hospital. And yes, you have got the most experience at robberies, but you also have the most experience in going to jail for robbery, and that's not something I'm trying to compete with you on. How is Mr Salt going to carry on paying for his wife's treatment if the police are watching us all and monitoring how much money he's spending? If we're suspected and have to go on the run he can hardly take his wife with him if she's sick in a hospital bed. You've got a respectable job now, you've gone straight. You need to focus on that and save yourself from further trouble. And also save the homes of Mrs Khamgenn and Mr Navey from yourself as well."

Kheng looked on in frustration at Meebor. Meebor knew this operation was about helping Salt's wife, and about the dream. It had all been explained and discussed before they got inside the bank. Meebor was wrong. Kheng was following the guidance of the spirits that had visited him. This was not a simple act of petty theft. It was about doing the right thing, harnessing positive energy. After all of the effort to get into the safe room, now was not the time for a big change of plan.

"Well I may have gone down for a few burglaries, but I didn't go down for murdering someone. Before we all decide that only Mr Salt is worthy of this incredible windfall, let's all ask ourselves why he's so strapped for cash and not able to support his family properly in the first place. Yeah, okay, so I ended up in the clink because I was poor. Salt was in there because he killed a man!"

Mr Salt let out an exasperated sigh.

"He's right you know, Mr Kheng. You've been a law abiding citizen all of your life. You served your country.

Now you have the most amazing chance. You can make the rest of your time so much easier. Live in comfort. You should get as much as you can out of this. Don't worry about me."

"Well, Salt, that's not how the dream worked, if you remember? I'm only in this because of the dream. There was the tree and wild boar forest spirit, the triangle for the number three, and the full moon, and the drips of gold, but just the drips of warm gold, not an entire moon-full of gold that would burn us. We're only here for the drips. Enough to make everything all right with Mrs Salt."

Meebor wasn't convinced:

"And what about your Aunty 'K' then?"

Meebor shone the light again at Kheng, forcing him to hold up his hand to shield his eyes.

"Where does you Aunt 'K' fit into all of this? Currently she seems a bit absent from the interpretation of the dream story. She sounds to me like she was a fiery old battle-axe. She probably would have wanted you to take as much of this cash as you can. Invest in a lifetime supply of whisky and lay around all day getting drunk. Have you thought about that? I'm just not sure I trust you. Either of you. We hardly know each other. You got me here to show you how to climb into the safe room, and now you want me to leave with nothing! You and Salt are probably planning to come back once I've gone and then take it all!"

"All right, Meebor. Fine. Get that light out of my face, will you. This bickering isn't getting us anywhere. We're going round in circles. I suggest we should sit down and discuss this calmly. And stop waving that torch around. There might be someone daft enough to be wandering around in this storm who passes by and starts to question why there's a light being waved manically around inside the bank and the sound of people arguing. Right now we leave the money exactly where it is. All of it. It's not going anywhere until the bank opens again. Agreed? Sit down and I'll tell you who my Aunty Kaylin was. Maybe you'll feel like you know me a bit better afterwards as well."

Meebor shook his head in bewilderment.

"We're already in this together. The only way you can cut me out of the money is by killing me. Maybe that's why Mr Salt is part of this robbery. That is his specialty after all."

After a brief period where nobody spoke, Meebor picked up the sack of money that he'd dropped. Noisily he put the sack back where he'd found it. He used the rustling of notes and the thud of the re-dropping to show he was disgruntled, as the darkness prevented him from communicating this with his facial expressions. Kheng was the first to sit down on the safe room floor, Mr Salt followed. Eventually, feeling he had delayed enough to make his point, Meebor joined them sitting cross-legged on the floor. The three men had resumed the same positions in which they had sat to make the oath.

"Well," said Meebor, "this has got to be the most ridiculous robbery I've ever been part of. Probably the most stupid bank heist in history. Sitting in my underpants, in the safe room of a bank, surrounded by cash, just so I can be told by you two why I'm not going to steal any of it on account of some eccentric relative. Go on then 'Mr Morals', tell us all what's so important about your Aunt Kaylin."

Kheng leaned back on his elbows and stared up through the bars of the high window. The rain had slowed to a gentle patter and the moon was starting to show again as the clouds cleared. It was bright tonight and seemed to have positioned itself just right so as to shine down onto their deliberations, and spur him on with their mission.

This time of year the moon always seemed a bit bigger. It reminded him of when he was a boy in the village and his mother had shown him how, if he squinted at it hard enough, the shadows in the moon looked like a giant rabbit. His neighbour said it was more like a woman standing under a tree pounding rice with a long pole. He could only really see the rabbit. Kheng pulled himself up from his elbows, returning to an upright sitting position. He looked at Salt and Meebor before taking a deep breath.

"My Aunt Kaylin was my father's oldest sister."

Kheng looked at his co-conspirators to be sure he had their attention, and then began to share his story.

35. Still no Sleep

Mr Tann was once again lying wide awake in bed, staring through the open shutters at the large full moon. It was just starting to move into view; now that the rain had stopped its light was quite vivid, casting moon-shadows of the window frame across the far wall of the room. In the distance he could hear a drum banging at the temple, in recognition that the waxing moon had achieved its task.

Stealing the money from the safe room was supposed to end Mr Tann's torment of sleepless nights, not add to them. The original intent to extract the cash without suspicion had gone rather well and he had congratulated himself several times when reviewing the facts of his theft in his mind. However, a restless sleep can be tormenting, and small problems can start to become major and irrational worries. He imagined what would happen if he were accused directly of taking the money. Would his poker face hold or would he collapse into a babbling confession? What if Hua Lin had marked the notes in some way to try to catch him out? What if Yeo-bo saw him leaving the safe room and remembered that he had no specific reason to be there? Guilt was being magnified by his insomnia and manifesting itself as an uncontrollable ache in the pit of his stomach.

One of his biggest worries was that he had unfortunately added the unforeseen complication of a meeting with his boss the next morning so that he could present his ideas on how to redesign and retrofit the safe room. Right now he had no ideas. He'd not slept properly for weeks. A recent history of insomnia was no basis on which to develop innovative plans. On top of that, Mr Hua Lin had seen him coming out of the safe room. The combination of the potential discovery of missing money and the fact that his alibi was based on a safe room design that didn't exist was not really helping to settle Mr Tann's peace of mind. These kinds of worries always seemed far worse when he was exhausted and trying to get to sleep – knowing that he was being irrational due to sleep deprivation didn't help either.

Mr Tann rolled out of bed, wrapped a large scarf around his middle, and wandered across the room to the bed where his wife lay and then shook her awake.

"Mrs Tann. We have a family emergency. You need to phone up your sister and get that builder husband of hers round here. Before I go to work tomorrow, I need to have come up with a new design for the provincial bank's safe room. If I don't have some designs to present then the consequences could be pretty bad for all of us!"

36. Kheng's Aunt Kaylin

"I was thirteen years old when Aunt Kaylin came to stay. She just arrived in the village one day, and there she was, part of the household. She was family. Family can just turn up and stay, and that's how it is. You never turn away your family. We made space for her and my father treated her like she was any other adult in the household. Except that she wasn't. She helped a bit in the rice fields, but never really did anything or made a contribution that compared to the efforts of my mother or her sisters. As Aunt Kaylin was spending less time in the fields, it was assumed that she was helping more with taking care of the children. I was the oldest, and I had two brothers and three sisters. She was mean to them, and to me, so I ended up taking care of the little ones most of the time. If one of them started to cry then she would beat them to make them stop. I would have to find a way to sneak them out of the house and use compounds from the plants in the forest to rub on their sores so that they felt less pain. My mother and her sisters assumed that Aunt Kaylin was watching over us so paid less attention to the children. They were hoping for a good harvest that year and spent days at a time in the rice fields, sleeping in a small hut on the hill beside the paddy. My father was usually out hunting for most of the day and didn't have time to check on the children when he got back. I made sure that any bruising from the beating was kept hidden so that no one asked questions which would inevitably lead to more beatings.

"In the afternoons, Aunt Kaylin used to drink the local wine. She used to drink it in the mornings as well, sometimes. My father had jars of wine brewing at the back of the house. She would start after the other adults had gone to the fields. Then she would get a bit drunk. It would lead her to get angry and hit the children.

"One day, she realised that the jar of alcohol that she'd been discreetly drinking from was becoming almost empty. She didn't want to be the one to empty it completely as my father would start to question where it had all gone. She called me up to the house, handed some money to me, and told me to go to the market in town and buy her a bottle of local whisky. She said that I needed to get back quickly, or there'd be trouble. I knew what that meant. My younger brothers and sisters would get a thrashing. The problem was that I wasn't allowed by my parents to walk all the way to the market on my own. It was in the town a couple of kilometres down the hill and my parents didn't want me going there. We were children from the village, we were not streetwise enough to be in the town on our own. Besides, if I wasn't in school I should be working in the family's fields and helping in the house.

"I quickly thought about it and decided that if I ran I probably had just enough time to make it into town, buy the whisky and get back before my father returned from hunting. Normally he'd get home in the early evening to give the women of the house time to prepare and cook whatever he'd caught that day.

"Aunt Kaylin told me she expected to get some change out of the money she'd given me. I didn't know what whisky cost, I'd never bought it before, but I took the money as I needed to hurry. I ran all the way to the town. It took me over an hour to reach it. I got to the market and started to look around.

"It was a large open-air country town market, busy and confusing to a village lad like myself. At the front were lots of local villagers who had come down for the day to sell what they had gathered from their farms. Mostly there were local vegetables and forest roots laid out on mats for people to buy. Behind them were the regular market vendors, selling rice from large baskets, green vegetables and seasonal fruits. To the side was the area where they sold fresh meat. Thick tables displayed hunks of raw meat from buffaloes and wild boar, whilst owners wafted at the flesh half-heartedly to reduce the swarm of flies that crowded over them. Beyond that were the small wild animals that had been caught in the forest, their legs bound, still alive so that the meat would be fresh for the buyers. Beneath the tables were baskets with live chickens ready for sale. The stalls that were deeper inside the market were the more permanent ones where they sold cooking oils, salt, kitchenware, farming tools and so on. I didn't really know my way around, so I decided this was the part of the market where I was most likely to find whisky, and made my way inside.

"I found a stall that had local whisky in glass bottles. I asked for a bottle but the man didn't want to sell me any. The owner was a wiry and slightly aggressive man. He told me to keep on going, whisky was no drink for a kid like me. He didn't want to hear that I'd been sent to buy it by an adult from my family in the village. The second stall owner was not too bothered, once I'd made up an excuse and said that my father had sent me because he was sick and so couldn't make it to town himself. The owner of the stall told me how much it cost. The price of the whisky was almost double the amount of the money that Aunt Kaylin had given me. I asked at another stall and at another. The story was the same. There was no way I could buy the local whisky with the money I had, and time was running out. I needed to get home. First I needed to calm Aunt Kaylin down so she didn't hurt my family, secondly I had to be back from town before my father found I had gone.

"I panicked. I went back to the first stall that I had asked at. It was two tables long and had many different types of goods, so I guessed that the owner was one of the richer ones at the market. I waited until I thought he wasn't watching. I then rushed behind the table, grabbed the first bottle of whisky and tried to run as fast as I could out of the market. There had been an old woman tending the vegetable stall nearby and she saw me. She started yelling out: 'Thief! Thief! Stop him!'

"Soon I had all the stall holders from the market chasing me and trying to grab me. I was thirteen years old and so fairly nimble, even if I wasn't quite as small as my brothers and sisters. I was diving under tables, and knocking into people, causing them to drop the things they'd just bought. I almost made it out. I was near the main entrance and made a dash for it, just as a woman selling broom-grass saw me running out with the mob of stall holders giving chase. She stuck a broom stick into my legs as I ran forward. I fell. I fell on my face. The bottle smashed underneath me. Shards of glass cut into my flesh, stinging all the more for the strong alcohol rubbing into the raw wounds. A couple of guys grabbed me and pulled me to my feet. People from the market were jeering at me. The store owner I'd stolen from was yelling at me, whilst giving a piece of his mind to the crowd that was gathering. I was dragged across the district town to the police station.

I was exhausted from having run to the town, the chase in the market, the fall, and the injuries. Despite the state I was in, they made me stand up against a wall at the back of the police station and wait. My legs were shaking with the pain of having to stand for so long, but I dared not sit for fear of the beating I imagined I would get. The sergeant then sent one of his men to go to the village and fetch my father.

"It seemed like hours later when my father eventually appeared at the station. He was furious and demanded an explanation. I didn't have one. If I told the truth about Aunt Kaylin taking the wine and sending me to town for the whisky, he might not believe me. It was just as likely, if not more so, that his thirteen year old son had wanted to get hold of some whisky to try it out with his school friends. If I told him about Aunt Kaylin I would undoubtedly inspire her to violently take her loss of face out on my sisters and brothers once my parents were back on the farm and away from the house. I kept quiet. I took the blame and I took a beating from my father for punishment.

"The next day, a captain from the army at the local barracks came to the house. He was a mean looking man. Meaner than the market stall owner I'd stolen from. He had hard dark eyes and an unforgiving stare. I'd seen him once before on a previous visit to town. He'd been getting drunk with some of his officers at a noodle shop and yelling at the quaking owner, telling him how bad his food was, bullying him as a show of strength to his men. I'd steered clear that day, but this time luck was not on my side.

"After the captain spent time talking with my father, I was called to the room to meet him. My mother was there as well, looking upset. I was told that I had become uncontrollable. My behaviour had embarrassed the family. My father was ashamed to send me to the village school. The only option he could see was that I should stop my schooling and join the army. At that time there was a desperate need in the country for more soldiers. The conflicts both outside the country and on the borders had taken their toll. It seems crazy looking back on this now, but I left my home that evening, and followed the captain back into town where the barracks were. I said goodbye to my mother and my brothers and sisters, and then off I went. A few days later, I was sent to a camp in the north of the country where they were training other young recruits. From then on I was army, and there was no going back. Within a few months I was supporting the other troops up on the border. I was a soldier on active duty, I wasn't a kid in a village any more, with a family, and a school. My childhood had ended right there.

"I think my Aunt Kaylin left the village about six months after that. Maybe she worried that I'd come back from the borders a bit tougher for the experience, wouldn't be such a pushover, and do something about the abuse she inflicted on us. She didn't come back. I remember hearing several years ago that she'd passed away. She'd been living with a man she'd met in a village near to Khoyleng. She'd died of some kind of natural causes. I didn't give it much thought at the time. I haven't thought of her since, until the dream that is.

"So, that's the story of my Aunt Kaylin. It's really a story of an innocent person being put in a situation where he is forced to become a thief. Not because he will benefit from the things he takes, but because it could have helped to protect the vulnerable from any more pain. I think that's why she's in the dream, although I hadn't really wanted to talk about all this out loud. It's about doing what is needed to protect someone that needs help. It's not about enjoying the spoils of the haul. That is why tonight should not be about robbing the entire bank. It's about doing just enough to support someone that desperately needs it. Now I know I failed when I was needed to help my brothers and sisters back then in the village, but this time I want to get it right. This isn't just about the money. It's about doing the thing that needs to be done. Maybe it'll make up for the time that I failed my brothers and sisters."

Kheng looked over at Meebor. Meebor was looking a little sympathetic. Possibly. It was hard to tell. The dim light from the torch was fading to almost nothing so there was just the light from the moon shining through the high window to help them see. Salt was looking on in awe at Kheng. He felt guilty that the conflict between the three of them had forced Kheng to share a painful history that he'd clearly rather have kept to himself.

Kheng cleared his throat:

"So then, Mr Meebor. Maybe it's time we heard your story? Tell us why you think you know all the answers when it comes to what's happening tonight."

37. The Two Man Job

"I'd been nicking stuff ever since I was a little kid. Small stuff. I had a kind of upper limit on the sort of job I would take on in one go, as a type of self-protection. My approach was to pinch enough to get by, but not enough to be in serious trouble. So at night I'd take a roosting chicken from the compound outside someone's house, or I'd wait for them to go to work, and then pull the mangoes and jackfruit from their trees and sell what I got at the roadside market. Kids' stuff – I was a kid. If I was feeling confident I'd try and get into people's houses and take their things. Just small things that were easy to pass on. Money, if I could. If someone saw me coming or going, and I was questioned later, it would be impossible to prove whose money it was. Possessions were different though. If they were valuable, then the owner would be trying hard to get them back. People had much less back in the day than they do now, so selling valuable stuff on wasn't easy, as people would wonder where it had come from. No, I had it all sorted. I'd spread myself thinly. Not taking too much from any one person. That way, if somebody caught me then I'd only done enough to mildly annoy them, but not enough for them to bother to pursue it through a police complaint. In fact, the police demanded a fee from them to fill in the complaint form and send it to the Superintendent to see if he was interested enough to follow up on it. So, it made more economic sense to be annoyed with me rather than turn me in. I was like this for most of my youth. It was my living. I'd steal enough to eat, pay for a few things, but nothing on a scale that would actually lift me out of poverty. However, it was then that I got mixed up with 'Tannoy Doi'.

"Tannoy was a small time criminal like myself. We actually met 'cos we were robbing the same place at the same time. I'd broken into the house of the District Administrator via a bathroom window, and Tannoy had come in through a gap under the eaves in the roof. We met in the corridor on the way to look for cash in the bedrooms. It was fairly clear how he'd earned his nickname of Tannoy. His exclamation of annoyance on finding that I was there robbing the place as well was loud enough to wake the whole street. I immediately scarpered back through the bathroom window and Tannoy followed me out of the building. Once we'd both legged it far enough, we stopped to catch our breath and had a bit of a laugh about it. It was the first networking I'd ever done as a burglar. Being an occupation that has to remain very low-key, it's quite difficult to meet fellow professionals, unless you're born into a family that's gone that way. Anyway, me and Tannoy became mates after that, and started working together.

"The key to working with Tannoy was to pick somewhere that it didn't matter if you made a noise. When he was a kid, their house had been next to the lamp-post with the public address system attached to it that belted out the news from five-thirty each morning. From an early age he'd just got used to talking loudly so he could be heard over the sound of the speakers giving the latest updates from the capital. It was a habit that he couldn't shake. Tannoy was a bit like me when it came to burglaries: going for easy pickings, and not taking risks. And, like me, he was starting to feel like it was time to scale things up and get himself out from the bottom of the pile. The trouble with the type of work that we were both in was that there was a lot of planning, staking out and taking risks. Overall though, we weren't any better off than other people with low paid jobs, but who had no particular risk of a run-in with the authorities. It was time to take things up a notch if the risk-taking was going to be worthwhile. By teaming up we had a new opportunity. For the first time, we could think about doing the type of robbery that was a two man job. It was time to find a more exclusive target with a bigger payout.

"The jobs I normally did involved sneaking around, casing a place to make sure it was empty and then striking when I knew no one was about. It took a lot of preparation, often for not much profit. With two of you working together, there was less need for all of that pre-planning. You could steal from under people's noses. One of you could be a distraction whilst the other one focused on swiping stuff. Tannoy, with his loud presence, was usually the distraction and I'd do the swiping. We started off doing a bit of pickpocketing in the provincial towns. Tannoy would approach someone, loudly asking about directions or pretending to be drunk, something like that, and I'd come in close behind them with my fingers in their bags taking out their purses or whatever they had.

"We soon learned that a better use of two people was for one of us to be a lookout whilst the other did the robbing. People are much less cautious about their stuff if they think they're only stepping out for a minute. It was easy enough to spot small shops on the street where the owner would pop out for ten minutes to get noodles. Normally they might just lock the door rather than pull down the shop front shutters or anything, sometimes not even bother with that. I'd pick the lock and then go inside and swipe all that I could while Tannoy watched out for their return. Normally there was an unlocked drawer at the top of the desk where they made their sales and it would be full of cash. Nobody believes they will be robbed. Even now, people happily assume that their neighbourhood is safe and filled with good people, and seem genuinely surprised when some crime befalls them.

"One time we got cocky and decided to rob the house of the police commissioner. It sounds more risky than it was. No one expected the police to get robbed so the duty officers were all standing outside the governor's house or monitoring the traffic. There was nobody for security at his place. We knew that the commissioner always played badminton with some government staff on a Friday evening. It was often announced on the community radio that he'd won some contest or other. Tannoy also knew that on his way to the sports hall each Friday he would drop his wife off to have her hair and make-up done, all ready for the weekend. Tannoy's sister-in-law worked at the hairdresser's and her conversation when she got back home was usually around who had been in to be beautified. As a result, Tannoy had a fairly solid knowledge of the comings and goings of the various well-to-do ladies of the town. Anyway, the point was that the house would be empty on a Friday evening for at least an hour. That gave us plenty of time to slip in, take the valuables, and make our get-away. Tannoy kept watch, just in case they came back. It was unlikely, but there might be a sudden emergency or security situation in the province which required a change of plan from the immediate routine. I shimmied up the drain pipe at the back of the house and got in through a bedroom window.

"From force of habit, I immediately went to the dresser and started rummaging around in the drawers for jewellery or money. It took me a while to notice, but in the end my attention was drawn to the commissioner's dress uniform, which was laid out on the bed. I guess he had some important function to attend later in the evening. I was young and immature and so my first instinct was to do something stupid like cut holes in it and hope he wouldn't notice until he turned up at the event and looked embarrassed. As my warped mind started scheming, my attention was eventually drawn to the large leather belt and holster. The holster had the commissioner's gun inside it. I guess you don't need to be heavily armed to play badminton, but it was a bit silly to leave the gun out in the house like that. However, like I said, the police commissioner was the last person expecting to get burgled. I took the gun and then went back through his drawers looking for the bullets. It took a while. I could hear Tannoy calling up at the window, wondering what I was messing about at. Normally this type of robbery didn't take that long. I wasn't leaving without the full set though, gun and bullets. Eventually I hit the jackpot. I found a small box of ammunition, underneath the bed, kept inside another metal box. Inside the metal box was a second gun.

"So, I returned to the window and dropped the bag with the jewellery and the guns down to Tannoy, shimmied down the drain pipe and we made our escape. It was the first time me or Tannoy had had access to guns. It was something of an opportunity. It would open the door to a whole new realm of criminal possibilities. It was not long after that we decided to get into highway robbery."

38. Highway Robbery

"Highway robbery, or at least the type we were going in for, was at a minimum a four person job. More was better really, but at least four on the job was essential.

"The way it worked was like this. You found a rural road, one in the provinces where there was lots of forest. You'd pick a route that people had to travel on but with stretches along the way with few or no houses at the roadside, just the bush. Deeper forest was better. You'd then wait for a bush taxi or car full of people to come along. You'd all wear hats, and then tie scarves to cover up the bottom part of your face so you couldn't be recognised or described later on to the authorities. One of the gang would then flag down the car, aiming a weapon at the driver. The people in the car were instructed to get out. These people were told to take off their outer clothes so they can be searched for money. You'd be surprised how many older women sew money into their clothing. It dates back to the old days when security was much worse than nowadays. The people being robbed were then taken by the second member of the gang about fifty metres out of the way into the forest where they would sit and be held as hostages, a kind of insurance policy in case the authorities accidentally stumbled across the proceedings. The third and fourth members of the team would then search through the belongings and bag up any loot they found. A second car comes along and you would do the same. Only this time, the people being robbed are just kept at gun-point on the ground by the side of the road. They are easier to control that way, and so are the original group of hostages. You have one of the crew stopping the cars, one watching the people that are being kept at the roadside, one sorting through the loot and one in the forest still with the hostages. Then after twenty minutes or so, once you've stopped a few more cars and have bagged up as much as the four of you can carry, you all disappear like shadows into the jungle. The people that you just robbed have to try and find their clothes again, which is a great way to give yourselves a head start should anyone be thinking of becoming rash and giving chase.

"Tannoy and I were only two people, so we recruited two more. My cousin, Duck-foot, had just been kicked out of secondary school at around that time. He seemed to be someone of suitably limited opportunities and with a low respect for the system, so I drafted him in. Tannoy followed suit. He had words with his younger brother, 'Bullhorn', so he came on board as well.

"The first time we robbed a vehicle we chose a fairly quiet provincial road to the south of Maklai. Our first car arrived at about two in the afternoon. We followed the plan. Tannoy held up the car and orchestrated the whole thing so that any bags and clothes people were wearing were dumped on the side of the road. It was the perfect job for Tannoy: someone who can only speak by shouting at you can be a bit intimidating in a hold-up situation. Once Tannoy had done his bit, I then took the hostages at gun-point into a clearing just inside the forest. Bullhorn and Duck-foot then set about searching all the belongings.

It all went perfectly. Then we waited. And we waited. We waited for half an hour and no other car came down the track. Not a motorbike, an old boy on a push-bike, a hardworking woman fetching firewood from her farm, nothing. It was embarrassing. I was stood there, holding these five hostages at gun-point, meanwhile they could see that the whole thing was a total wash out. It undermines you as a kidnapper when that sort of thing happens. I mean, you start off looking all imposing and powerful, and half an hour later on after standing around and kicking at stones and shuffling your feet, well, you're no longer commanding the kind of respect and fear that you need to intimidate a group of hostage detainees. Meanwhile the hostages start muttering to each other, and then one of them needs to take a pee. If you let the first one go to ease themselves then they all need to go. The control rapidly slips away. In the end, we gave it another hour and a half and then we split. It was starting to get dark by then and we had a couple of ks to do, finding our way through the forest to the track where we'd left our motos. Anyway, at least we'd had a practice, and the two younger guys had received a fairly easy introduction into the highway caper. It's easy to forget that Tannoy and I had enjoyed a lifetime of minor criminal activity leading up to the dizzying heights of armed highway robbery. Duck-foot and Bullhorn were just freshmen. A couple of days later we tried again, and chose a slightly busier road.

"The second robbery went much better. We stopped five cars: two private cars and three bush taxis. We did quite well out of it. People don't travel out to their villages in the provinces without taking gifts for their relatives or money to socialise with their friends, they need to put on a bit of a show on coming home. Meanwhile if you're heading out to the big city then you're taking your savings to do some spending on things you can't normally get. Either way is good if you're the one doing the robbery.

"After the fourth robbery we decided to take a break. There was a danger that the police would start to get a bit wise to what we were doing. Once you'd identified the best spots for this kind of thing there was a danger of falling into a bit of a routine, and that the police would be keeping an eye on those locations. Also, there was a good chance that the taxi drivers and travellers would start bringing guns in their cars if they knew the chances of being robbed were getting high. We were starting to make some serious money. The question was: where did would we go from there?"

39. Duck-foot's Bus

"Duck-foot had the initial idea. It wasn't bad for him, considering he wasn't really drafted onto the team to be the main ideas man. The brains of the set-up was usually Tannoy or me. Anyway, Duck-foot complained that the part of the robbery we couldn't control was when or how often the cars came round the corner to be stopped by the crew. You can't just pick and choose which cars to rob when everyone is stood at the side of the road in their underwear at gunpoint. If two cars come along at the same time, you can't just wave one past and stop the other 'cos it's more difficult to handle. We'd had a few dodgy moments when cars had come from two directions at the same time, and Bullhorn had had to stop the one while Tannoy did the other. It was risky 'cos we only had two guns, and one would be in the forest with the hostages. On the last robbery, we had four cars parked up when three other cars came round the corner at once. It had all got a bit chaotic, and in the panic, Tannoy had let off a shot from his pistol. We didn't stick around long after that, as you never know who you're going to alert: there might be some villagers hunting wildlife nearby in the forest who are feeling cocky enough to come and take you on.

"Anyway, Duck-foot's point was that we could always

control all of this randomness if we robbed just one vehicle. To make it worthwhile then, it needed to be one with a lot of people on it, so either a train, an aeroplane, or a bus. Of course the security around an airport was too much for a bunch of small time criminals like ourselves, and they were usually crawling with well-armed military back in those days. There were no trains operating at the time. They had all stopped during the war and the infrastructure had been damaged beyond repair. What did make an interesting prospect, however, was the bus.

"We spent a bit of time thinking on this one. There were less buses around in those days and they normally took the more travelled roads between the larger towns. Our usual M.O. of picking a secluded country road and lying in wait was not an option any more. The main roads all had houses built regularly along the sides so there were no really ideal isolated spots to follow the routine. Therefore, we needed to hijack the bus and then somehow divert it to a quiet spot so that we could get on with our work of robbing all the passengers uninterrupted. We spent about a week staking out various by-roads and options. In the end it was decided that we would rob a bus coming out of Maklai on the road going north to Fai-dan Province. Maklai was a more central trading town than Fai-dan. People on the bus would include traders and passengers who were either returning from selling their products in the markets and so cashed up, or those who had just spent their money on the type of expensive goods you couldn't get in Fai-dan. Either way, there would be a lot of valuable stuff for us to take. On top of that, the traders in Fai-dan usually paid the bus owners to fill up the floors with goods, as it was a cheap way to transport the stuff they needed to sell in their shops. The roof of the bus was usually hugely over-burdened with goods as well so it would look like a double-decker. This overloading was all to our benefit as the bus wouldn't be travelling very fast. However, as it was on its way out of Maklai it would be even slower as it had to climb the hill up to the plateau, and the driver would also be looking out for extra passengers that would be flagging down the bus as they wanted to travel north.

"This was the plan: Duck-foot and I would pretend to be passengers and flag down the ambling bus at the side of the road. Tannoy would be somewhere near by on a motorbike. Once we were in the bus he would follow behind as a sort of convoy. Just before we reached the planned turnoff, Duck-foot and I would hold up the driver at gunpoint, and divert the bus down a nearby quiet side-road. I would be in charge of managing the passengers. We'd decided to take the bus into an old palm tree plantation where they used to do palm oil. The company had given up years back so now it was overgrown and wasted. A couple of clicks down the road we would meet up with Bullhorn who would have already been waiting there, double-checking that there were no authorities about. The track didn't really go anywhere, to a village or anything, but it was best to be sure. Duck-foot would then tell the driver to pull over, the passengers would have to get out, and then after that it's a robbery like any other one. Timing-wise, we decided that we wanted to get on the bus at about two in the afternoon as any stray police would be sleeping off their mid-day fill of rice, and we'd have plenty of time to get it all done before it got dark.

"Anyway, we got everything set up, and waited part-way up the long hill road, ready to catch our bus. Sure enough, at about 1.20pm, a dilapidated old and rusty red bus came labouring painfully up the hill, straining with a full load of passengers and a roof piled high with hundreds of cabbages. Duck-foot stood out in the road and flagged it down. The bus stopped and, with our hats pulled down low over our faces, we got on through the open doorway, which was missing its door. In fact the driver's door and most of the windows were missing as well but this was not unusual for the old buses doing the slow runs, and it helped with airflow, to cool passengers, should the vehicle reach a sufficient speed to allow that to happen. We climbed up the gangway in the centre of the bus. I say climbed, the entire floor of the bus was packed as usual with cardboard boxes and crates. Most of it seemed to be boxes of noodles, tinned fish, cartons of drink, or kitchenware, that sort of thing. Where passengers had seats, their legs were on boxes, so they were more squatting uncomfortably than actually sitting. Down the middle, was a row of plastic stools with people sitting on them, perched on top of all the boxes of food. Once we were in, we stood at the front end of the gangway and held onto the luggage rack to steady ourselves. The bus shuddered forward, creaking uneasily under the immense weight of cabbages that were attached to the full length of the roof, piled almost high enough to be a second deck. To be honest, seeing the beast lumbering up the road with all the vegetables on the roof didn't make it my first choice of bus to hijack. It was possible the next bus would have something of a higher value on the roof like new motorbikes. However, Duck-foot reminded me of the time schedule, and that Bullhorn was waiting for us in the old palm-oil plantation. There was no predicting when the next bus would be. It might be ten minutes away or two hours, and even then it might not have as many passengers as this one. Duck-foot was itching to get started, so I thought it best to go along with it.

"I could see that Tannoy had pulled out from his position near the noodle shop on the other side of the road.

He was on a motorbike and riding just behind us. We got near the turning for the plantation. Duck-foot pulled his scarf up around his face and I did the same. He then held the pistol at the driver and told him to turn off the road and down the track at the side. A woman sitting in the gangway perched on a plastic stool, balanced on some tinned prunes, screamed out. I got the second gun from inside my jacket and pointed it at the passengers, telling them to stay seated and be quiet. The woman, and some of the others, looked fairly terrified, but it did the job. Looking back it's not something I'm terribly proud of. How could you be proud of scaring someone like that? But those were the times. You did what you did to survive and we weren't setting out to hurt anyone, only to steal. We just wanted to have enough, same as other folks.

"The bus driver was really scared. He broke wind loudly and began sweating profusely. However, he managed to do as Duck-foot had instructed, and the bus turned off the main road and headed into the old plantation.

"Now that we were off the main road we were no longer climbing, and the bus was able to gain a bit of momentum. Looking back, I think this is where the problems started. The driver was panicking. He was more focused on the weapon that Duck-foot had pulled on him than on looking at the road. He failed to notice an enormous hole in the old plantation track and he hit it full-on and hard with the front left wheel. Everyone who was sitting down was thrown up in the air by the jolt impacting on the bus. A few of the more precarious people in the gangway on plastic stools fell from their perches. However, the biggest impact was that Duck-foot lost his balance, banged his head on the corner of the luggage rack and his gun went off. The driver yelled out in pain as the bullet flew through his leg. He grabbed his leg, and, what with the pain, the jolt, and the surprise at being shot, he fell right out of the bus, through the missing driver's door. The bus veered sharply to the driver's side and headed down into the deep ditch at the side of the track. It hit the ground at the bottom of the drainage ditch with a heavy smack, leaving the bus pivoted sideways to the road with the back end up in the air. The engine was revving wildly as Duck-foot had fallen into the driver's foot-well during the accident and had his elbow on the accelerator. I, meanwhile, had been thrown violently forward. My back had landed hard against the already cracked windshield. In that slow-motion spilt second I could feel the glass shattering, and the first pieces raining onto the ground behind me. At the same time a load of boxes fell forward onto me. I was pushed out through the broken windshield and onto the ground behind me, the boxes trapping my lower body. I looked to the side and could see the driver was still near to the bus, trying to crawl away slowly and painfully. However, he was soon to learn the consequences of overloading his bus that day. The netting securing the cabbages on the roof had come loose and, slowly at first, they started falling down. Soon the cascade of produce gained momentum, flooding down into the ditch and the driver gradually disappeared beneath a heavy mountain of leafy vegetables. I lay there for what seemed an eternity, my gun still in my hand pointing up through the broken window at the stunned passengers, listening to the constant thud of cabbage on cabbage as they continued to rain down.

"Soon enough, Tannoy was next to the bus at my side. He dug my legs out from the boxes and dragged me out of the ditch, a little way from the scene of the accident. As I sat on the side of the track, it was clear to me that my left leg was broken. The pain was incredible. Meanwhile,

Tannoy was back on the bus, pulling Duck-foot from under the foot-well and out on to the side of the track as well.

"Whilst we were focusing on sorting ourselves out, we'd failed to pay attention to what was happening at the back of the bus. A number of passengers were climbing out of the back window and re-grouping for a counterattack. It turned out that over the weekend there had been a police convention of sorts in Maklai, and a few of the participants were travelling back to Fai-dan Province by bus. I had been more focused on the screaming woman at the front of the bus. I'd failed to note the somewhat calmer group of men towards the back. They were quick to realise that the gun that some idiot on the bus was waving at them was a police issue revolver and so, although calm, they were incensed. There were extra commendations up for grabs if they were able to recover a couple of those guns. It didn't take them long to overpower us. They had a couple of guns on them as well. I was immobilised with the broken leg, Duck-foot was barely conscious. It was lucky for Bullhorn though. We were so far from reaching where we'd agreed to meet, that, once Bullhorn had decided to see if the distant gunshot was anything to do with us, we were already in police custody and the passengers were walking back to the main road. He found the knackered bus still with its back end in the air.

"The driver, who had been completely forgotten, had regained consciousness and was calling out from beneath all the vegetables. Bullhorn dug him out, tied his scarf around the shot-up leg to reduce the bleeding, and then used his motorbike to take him to a health centre that was a few kilometres away, back on the main road. He didn't hang around after that of course. I suppose it was one good thing from the whole affair that the poor guy didn't bleed to death whilst entombed beneath the cabbages. Armed robbery was going to result in a tough enough sentence from the authorities. A sentence for murder was too much to begin to think about.

"Tannoy, Duck-foot and I all went down for armed robbery and hijacking. Of course, Tannoy and I were also done for robbing the police commissioner's house: there was irrefutable evidence based on the guns which they recovered from us. The police didn't go lightly with us on that one. To them it was more serious than the hijacking. I did more than ten years' hard labour for what basically amounted to not quite robbing a bus full of cabbages.

"So, Mr Kheng, there is the case for the prosecution. I learned long ago that once you go down this road, the stakes are high, and you can lose everything you've got. You might justify to yourself that you are only taking just enough. Well, that's sort of what we did. That argument didn't wash with the magistrates and the judge. What I learned is that if what you are risking is high, then you'd better make sure that what you're getting is worth it, and that you leave nothing behind."

40. Karaoke

On the other side of town Mr Hua Lin was sitting with the Liangtok family, staring at his bottle of imported beer. He'd just crooned a beautiful love song aimed in the direction of Liangtok's daughter, Dae-gee. It was a song that he'd understood to be beautiful anyway, as it was a cheesy ballad about a guy who'd fallen in love but his best friend had got hold of the girl in question before he had the chance to make his move, and so he was all moody and upset about it. Dae-gee had ignored his performance for the most part. This was surprising as it seemed to be about as emotionally charged and moving as karaoke could get and he'd crooned with a passion and style that was rarely found outside of Khoyleng. Perhaps he'd misjudged the ability of those raised in the rural provinces to grasp the subtle poignancy of the heart-breaking lyrics. When Dae-gee's attention hadn't been captivated by cooing with her girlfriend over their various expensive jewellery, she had been watching Keht, the twenty-something year old guy with a very gelled quiff who was the son of one of Liangtok's associates. Hua Lin had returned the microphone to a muted appreciation from the audience, and Mr Liangtok had mocked him about how he should learn to sing and how lucky it was that he had his day job at the bank. It was a joke of course, but it hadn't helped ingratiate Hua Lin with the daughter. Keht was now on the small stage, gyrating his hips like a speeding lizard, and posing like a rock star with his ridiculous gelled up mountain of hair that he sculpted to try to look like the hero from an anime cartoon. Dae-gee's attention was well and truly held as Keht strutted around, weaving like some professional dancer, and pouting like he was playing to a stadium of spellbound teenage fanatics. Hua Lin almost started to feel impressed himself, before he reminded himself that Keht was the competition and he was there on a mission to beat Keht to the girl. It wasn't a mission he could particularly afford to lose either. He was literally there on 'borrowed' money, if not actually borrowed time.

Hua Lin stared at his bottle of beer and started picking at the label. He knew that he needed to come up with a quick plan to get Keht out of the way and grab the attention of Dae-gee. However, watching from the sidelines while Liangtok's daughter giggled with her privileged expensive friends and Keht showed off his toned muscles didn't provide him with the boost he needed for inspiration. Besides, he was totally broke, so there wouldn't be many more chances to play at being one of the big men in town, hanging out with the wealthy and powerful, and posing as the indisputable best option for a rich man looking to marry off his daughter. In fact it was worse than that. He'd stolen the bank's money that he was supposed to protect, just to fund his right 'to sit at the table'. Even then, that money was barely going to cover his costs for the evening. When Mr Liangtok and his cronies went out on the town, they did so in the most expensive way. They always chose the most expensive restaurant, the most expensive food, the most expensive party. It was because they needed to be seen by others to have the cash, rather than to actually enjoy their wealth. It was also, as was currently being proven to Hua Lin, to single out Liangtok's peers from those who couldn't keep up. It was a system that allowed other rich businessmen with interests in town to quickly find out who had the most wealth and influence and with whom to make future business partnerships. It meant people with aspirations had no doubt about the pecking order and where to start ingratiating themselves.

Hua Lin was fed up. He felt it was clear that Mr Liangtok was tolerating him as he was his bank manager and oversaw his business accounts. This meant that Mr Liangtok saw their relationship as something that was marginally useful to foster in case of some future cash flow problem or if there was a need for banking services outside of usual opening hours or accepted rules. Meanwhile, Hua Lin was clearly of no interest to Dae-gee. She was evidently more into the rippling six-pack rock star type than the safe and dependable bank manager type. Who could blame her? Her father was already her personal bank manager, she didn't need another person to provide her with financial stability. Keht, however, was an exciting good-looking adventure until the next one came along.

Hua Lin finished peeling off the label from the back of the beer and brushed the torn pieces of paper from the table and onto the floor. Maybe he should feel relieved. Failing to enchant Liangtok's daughter was really a lucky escape. Dae-gee would be a difficult girl to hold on to, even if he did get her attention in the short term. She wasn't exactly going to bring any joy to his life, just the extra cash via Daddy. It didn't stop him from feeling fed up though. He was broke, he was a criminal stealing from his own bank, and was now out of funds to progress his career and live up to his own expectations. He'd thought coming to the province was a great opportunity to turn things around, to fast-track himself into the executive club of the wealthy and powerful. He looked at himself in the mirror that was on the other side the dance floor. He had hoped to see a sharp big-city banker who was hanging out in the provinces, sharing his slick city moves to impress the local wannabes so they could see what they were missing out on in the big leagues. All he saw was a small time young and inexperienced guy in a suit. He was out of place, not because he was the big man from the city. It was because in Maklai he didn't really have the history, the family connections or the money to justify his right to be the equal of the people who really had the money to be there. He also saw a foolish man who'd just stolen from his own bank and whose only plan to undo his act of criminality was to get cashed up by marrying the dizzy airhead that was currently sitting across from him, smooching with rock-star-Keht and messing with his stupid quiff. For the first time since he'd arrived in Maklai, Hua Lin's self-confidence was beginning to waver. He could see that his life was about to get really difficult, and right now he couldn't see any way of digging himself out.

41. Mr. Salt's brother, Somveat

There was a long pause before Mr Salt began his story. It was a hesitation which conjured up memories that Salt had buried deep within him. Ones that he did not want to face.

"We used to play this game in the village. The boys and the girls were always shy to talk to each other, and it was improper for a girl to be on her own with a boy from another household. But if you were in a group then it was okay. The boys would be on one side. The girls would be on the other. A scarf was rolled up into a ball. It was then thrown at the other group. If they caught it then they would throw it back, but if it hit someone and fell to the ground then that group had to dance for the others while they sang. For the boys it was basically just a way to show off to the girls, and for the girls I guess a way to decide if they liked the boys. There was a girl in the village I really liked, called Vilay. Their family had some small farmland next to where our family grew rice. She had beautiful long hair and she was always kind. If their mango tree had fruit, sometimes she'd share some with our family as we didn't have any. Because her family's upland farm was near to ours, during the harvest or planting season when the children had to help more than usual, I would often find I was walking down the same track as her and we'd get to talk.

"It was the day after New Year. I would have been about fifteen. All the adults were sleeping off the rice wine from the day before, and the children of the village started playing the scarf game. My brother was only about a year older than me and he was playing as well. I tried hard to get the rolled up scarf, and eventually I'd caught it and was my turn. I threw it back at Vilay. She missed catching it and so it hit her and fell to the ground. She and the others had to do a dance. Even at that adolescent age, I knew that it was as sure a signal I would ever get that she was interested in me. She could have caught the scarf if she'd wanted to. I knew that marriages were more complicated than just two people wanting to be together, and that parents had to negotiate. I also knew that if the children were really determined that they wanted to be together then they could influence those decisions. I'd never felt so happy in my life when Vilay dropped that scarf and the way she looked at me afterwards. After they danced, Vilay threw the rolled up scarf back at the boys and my brother, Somveat, jostled to catch it. He got it and then threw it back hard towards Vilay. She caught it easily. I knew then for sure that the first time she missed the scarf she had done so on purpose. My brother got more and more determined to catch the scarf. Each time he got it, he threw the scarf straight back at Vilay, and each time she caught it and returned it to the boys, not taking any notice of my brother.

"My brother and I stopped talking to each other after that. He was jealous. He could see that Vilay preferred me to him. I often question how much of his anger was because I was his younger brother and was getting the attention that he wanted. Maybe he felt it was his right to choose her because he was the oldest. I'd wonder if his reaction would have been so extreme if it was one of the older boys in the village that caught her interest. But it was crazy, me and my brother were silently fighting over a girl that neither of us had the slightest claim over. Our parents didn't help. They thought that Vilay's family were lower class and not as well-off as ours. Vilay's family had four girls and her parents had never had any boys. This was considered back luck, and my parents didn't want either of their boys involved with their family. The benefits would be less than they could get elsewhere because Vilay's family would have to provide for four daughters who would eventually live with their husband's families, so they would have less labour to work the land. The eventual inheritance would be a much smaller scrap of land than our own family had, and it would be on the same steep-sided hillside which was so much more difficult to farm rice. At the start of that harvest season, we went to sleep in the fields, as we did every year, to protect the crop and harvest the rice as it became ready. My father told us to build a small temporary hut out of bamboo on high stilts, so we could sleep there and use the vantage point to keep watch over the fields. Imagine, two brothers trying to coordinate building a thing like that without speaking a word to each other. It was terrible. I loved Vilay, but I loved my brother too. We'd grown up so close together, playing, working on the farm, making mischief. As we put the final piece of thatched roof on the top of our bamboo sentry post, my brother finally spoke to me. 'I will get her, you know I will,' he said. 'She may like you more but I'm the older brother. I will marry first, our father will expect this, and I will make sure I get both ours and Vilay's parents' consent. You'll have to watch her marry me and live with it.' I was furious. I was a kid with mixed-up emotions. I'd not shared two words with my brother for months, and now this. 'I hate you,' I cried, and charged at him with all my strength and anger. Grappling, we fell through the makeshift side of the look-out hut and tumbled all the way to the ground. I staggered to my feet, ready to fight my brother and take whatever punishment he could give. He was bigger than me, and no one at school had ever been brave enough to take him on, but I didn't care. In that moment I was ready to take a beating if that was what it took to sort this out. And as I stood there, fists clenched, trembling with adrenalin, I looked down at my brother. He just lay there, motionless. I kicked his legs and yelled at him to get up and fight me. But there was nothing. I bent over him to see what was wrong. Blood was coming from his head where he had landed on a large rock. I tried to sit him up and his head fell back; his neck was broken.

"I wept. The last thing I'd said to my brother was that I'd hated him. Now he was dead. I'd killed him. I sat there for a while, holding him. Maybe he was just unconscious. I couldn't believe he was really dead. He'd come round again and everything would be all right. But he didn't. The sun was getting lower in the sky, and we would be expected home soon, so I climbed back up the ladder to the look-out hut and quickly replaced the broken bamboo. Then I carried my brother's body down in the forest by the stream. I returned to the hut, took the bamboo ladder that was against the side and laid it up against a tree near the stream. Somehow, I found the strength to pull my brother's body up the ladder. I heaved with all the energy I could find, and eventually got high enough to where there was a fork in the trunk of the tree. I made sure the body wouldn't fall and then I left him there. I didn't want to bury him. I was too scared. Somehow I still believed that he was going to wake up and everything would be all right. It was dark by now. I washed my brother's blood from my hands and my shirt in the stream. Then I put the ladder back against the hut and started to walk up through the tracks and back to the village. I told my mother that I'd not seen my brother Somveat all afternoon, and so decided that I should stay and eat in the house rather than be alone in the fields. She was so annoyed that Somveat hadn't stayed with me. She was annoyed with both of us. She knew we weren't talking to each other, so she assumed that we'd not been together on account of our feud.

"The next morning, as there was still no sign of my brother, before breakfast my father and my two uncles went to the farm to look for him. They reached the fields where the hut was and saw the blood on the rock where my brother's head had cracked open. They asked me about it but I said nothing. More villagers joined in the search. It wasn't long before my uncle's hunting dogs started barking at the tree in the forest near the stream, and then they found the body.

"My father was devastated. He couldn't look at me. My uncle asked me what happened and I told him the truth. But I'd lied the day before about what had happened and I don't think they knew what to believe. I was brought before the village leader, and on hearing the story he said that he had to inform the police. I was arrested and taken from the village. That wasn't the worst of it though. My family and my family's land had become taboo. We had angered the spirits in the forest and brought bad luck on the village. Sometimes when that happened the whole village had to move to a new site in the forest and start again. The village leader and the elders held a meeting. They decided that my family would have to be banished from the village. The few buffalo that my parents owned would have to be sacrificed to order to try to calm the forest spirits and seek their absolution for the wicked act I had performed in their lands. Our family's land was believed to have become very unlucky and no other villager was allowed to use it. The next day my parents left the village with only the possessions that they could carry. They had lost their home, their lands and their eldest son. In their minds they had also lost their second son. They never spoke to me again."

42. Vilay

Salt looked up from the corner of the room and leaned back against a pile of money sacks to steady himself. Tears were streaming from his eyes.

"I had no idea, Salt," said Meebor.

Meebor sat attentively, looking penitent for his previously low opinion of Mr Salt.

"Maybe we should get you some of your coffee before we continue," offered Kheng.

Kheng could see the effort of telling his story had drained Mr Salt's energy. Meebor got up, stood on the table and eased his way up into the ceiling. A few moments later he had returned with the coffee and the cups.

Kheng took the flask from him and placed the cups on the floor, carefully pouring to make sure nothing dripped and left evidence of their entry into the bank. He passed one of the hot brews to Meebor and then another to Salt.

"So, how did you find out about your parents and the land? Surely by then you had been taken by the authorities?" asked Kheng.

"Vilay came to visit me in prison, later. Much later, after things had calmed down a little. She told me everything. How she had watched from under her house as my parents slowly walked out of the village, pushing an old wooden cart with their clothes and few possessions piled on, trying to get to the district town.

"I was taken straight to the provincial town police headquarters. It was treated as murder you see. The village leader knew about the conflict between Somveat and myself. There are no secrets in a small village. So the story that was told was one of two brothers feuding over a girl, and one of the brothers, in his rage, kills the other one. Even the truth that I'd told my uncle wasn't so far from that. In my anger I'd attacked him and he was dead. Who could prove that his death was an accident? There were no witnesses and I'd tried to cover up the deed. I was taken before the provincial magistrate, and the village leader and my uncle both had to give evidence. Even though I'd admitted to the accident, I was found guilty of murdering my brother and given a prison sentence. A few days later I was transferred from the cells in the police station and taken to a prison in the next province. We were used for hard labour. I was a young boy doing a man's work on child's rations. It was two years later that Vilay found me and persuaded the prison officers to let her see me. It was the most wonderful thing. For the first time since the accident I had hope. She believed my story and said she would wait for me, however long it took.

"It was another nineteen years before I got out of prison. It was a long time for me. It was forever. Time stops in a place like that. It was a long time for Vilay as well. She had spent all of her young life struggling to get by without a husband to support her. She moved to the same provincial town to get unskilled work in the factory. Eventually she got some training in operating the machines and moved up the ladder a little bit. Her family didn't want to know her any more as she was following me and I was bad luck. If she was waiting for me then she was bad luck too, and they didn't want her back in the village for fear of angering the spirits again. Vilay and I married shortly after I was released. We had our boy a year after that and the girl a year later. We were a bit old by then to have too many kids, so two was enough.

"So that's the whole story. Vilay gave up everything for me, and so now I have to do everything I can to get her through this illness. The problem is, Mr Meebor, if we take all the money and I get caught, then we'll lose each other all over again. I'm not a young man any more. I don't have the strength any more to keep waiting for a life that's being denied. If we take it all and then I have to go on the run, it's like Mr Kheng says, I still won't be with her at the hospital each day. It'll be almost as bad."

Meebor nodded.

"Fine. Don't think I don't know something about life in prison. I'm not in a big hurry to get back there either."

Kheng took a slurp of his coffee, which had now cooled sufficiently to be gulped rather than sipped.

"So let's agree on a compromise. How about Salt tells us how much we need to take to pay for his wife's hospital bills. We double that number and you get to keep the other half. I don't need anything for myself, I just need to follow this through and get Papa Han's tree spirit out of my head."

Meebor looked to the ground for a moment before looking up and nodding.

Kheng breathed a sigh of relief.

"So then, we are agreed. Now maybe we should finally get on with this bank robbery before the sun comes up."

The three of them slowly got to their feet, put the plastic bags they were using as gloves back on their hands, and in a slightly more subdued manner than earlier, they made their way over to the sacks filled with money.

43. Keys

The front gates made their usual apologetic shudder forwards, exhaling a rusty creak from the ancient hinges as they did so. The overnight rain had done nothing to lubricate the aging joints. The mild grinding noise had become a long established phrase in the morning chorus and did not disturb the chirps of the sparrows or the heartfelt efforts of neighbouring cockerels. Mr Tann shuffled listlessly through the opening until he gradually arrived at the front door of the bank. Meebor watched him perform this apathetic routine as he held the gate back for him and placed a stone in front of it to stop it from creaking closed again.

"Morning, Mr Tann. A bit fresh, eh? All that rain last night. All rather unexpected, but I'm glad I wasn't out here sitting in it. I was safe at home, sleeping in my bed."

Mr Tann glanced back at Meebor. He wasn't sure about this new guard. He was a bit too cocky, always sounded like he was trying to sell you something.

Mr Tann rooted around in his battered old leather satchel and searched for the over-size bunch of keys that formed the hub of all bank security, before replying in the absent way that had developed from Kheng's long held routine.

"Good morning, Mr Meebor. Everything okay?"

"Yes, Mr Tann. No problems at all. All nice and quiet here. Nothing going on."

Mr Tann looked up at Meebor in a particularly vacant and tired sort of way.

"Always good to know."

Meebor noticed that Mr Tann was looking worn out, somehow more vulnerable than usual. It was the sort of tiredness that builds up over time and is difficult to recover from.

Mr Tann looked back down at his weather-beaten satchel and returned to his rummaging. It was made particularly cumbersome by the large roll of papers that were sticking out of the top corner of his satchel, and seemed determined to fall to the floor should he make any attempt to put his hand inside the bag. Having at last located the mammoth clump of keys, he then rifled through the largely redundant collection of openers for the one that would persuade the front door to swing forward and let him in. Mr Tann had been performing this duty with tireless regularity for years, and in all that time he'd never managed to hit upon the right key with any level of precision or efficiency. However, today the frustration at failing to adequately perform his first task of the morning was even more evident from his tired and wan expression. Meebor concluded that the events over recent weeks had taken their toll on the old man.

He looked on with a degree of sympathy as the head clerk began a second review of the impossibly full key ring, holding on to one of the bigger keys and trying to work his way from there, without losing track of which ones had already been studied and rejected. Meebor's passive concern for the disillusioned man and his challenge with this basic task was probably slightly more genuine than usual. It was rare that his well-practised level of apathy would waiver. However, the irony was not lost on him. The previous night he'd robbed the bank by using the key to walk in through the back door, the very same bank which was currently so stubbornly reluctant to provide any access to its head clerk. Meebor wondered whether the frail and dilapidated man that was rattling a collage of scrap metal at a seemingly unmoveable door was likely to notice the depletion of the vast wads of notes they had stored inside. Only time would tell. Of all the resources available to a guard for a bank in a sleepy provincial town, 'time' was the one that they had in abundance.

44. Cooking

Mr Hua Lin sat at his desk, facing Ms Win-Kham. Despite the blurriness of his sleep-deprived eyes, he could see that she was looking particularly attractive. Was it something new she'd done with her hair? It might be something she was wearing. Somehow she still remained appropriately prim for her office duties. Was it a new air of confidence about her, or was it just that she was also looking at him with genuine expression of concern.

"There is no mistake, Mr Hua Lin. I've counted all the money three times just to be sure. We are down over fifteen million nham."

It was true that Ms Win-Kham had counted the money three times. This was primarily because she had expected the difference between the ledger and the money in the safe room to amount to just under three million nham. However, this assumption was based entirely on the fact that she had cooked the books the day before so that this would be the case. Three million nham was not a small amount. Fifteen million was more than all their annual salaries combined. In her original plan, when she expected to have to steal some of the money she had been thinking around a sum of 200,000 nham. This was not an insignificant amount, but probably small enough to avoid prison time if caught. When she'd cooked the books she'd felt three million might be overdoing it a bit. However, if something was worth doing it was worth doing properly. If Hua Lin was indebted to her for a three million rescue then he would be more eager to rush them into matrimony to make sure he didn't let her out of his sight. Fifteen million, on the other hand, was a crazy amount to have got lost. The extra twelve million that she'd had to add to her own manipulation of the ledger was really helping her to maintain a genuine look of shock.

The three million of course was relatively easy to make disappear. She just had to put the books back how they should have been before she messed with them. Now she was almost regretting cooking the books at all. It seemed that she had wasted her time over the previous days as the books were already askew without any help from her. She could have implemented her plan to entwine her web around Hua Lin without having to do anything wrong at all. Trying to hide the extra twelve million would be a big challenge. It would be incredibly difficult to make the problem go away. However, originally she was expecting to do some creative bookwork when she was focusing on plan A, which had involved some minor stealing. She would just have to apply those principles on a much bigger scale. There was also the risk that a fifteen million nham cover up was so big that Hua Lin would lose his bottle and go straight to his supervisors, who would then call in the police. Of course, that didn't directly affect her, but it would spell the end of Hua Lin's career and, therefore, her chances of stepping up to a privileged lifestyle in the capital.

Hua Lin's reaction to the loss of fifteen million nham had also been one of genuine surprise and shock. His reation would no doubt be to his advantage, should it be recalled by Ms Win-Kham if called to the witness stand at a later date. Hua Lin had only taken about 100,000 nham from the safe room. It may even have been less than that. He'd not really counted at the time. Now it was irrelevant. It was not as if he had the chance to put it back. What on earth had happened to the rest? And when? He made regular checks of all the bank's systems and ledgers and had failed to notice anything like this.

The two sat in silence, staring at the documents for the cash count and the ledgers that Ms Win-Kham had put on the desk. Ms Win-Kham's expression was vacant, but her mind was working fast. Sure enough, she had the ability to doctor a few transactions and gradually make the balances change, but this would never be enough. It would take her months, based on her level of access to documentation, to cover up this kind of money. She looked up at Hua Lin and realised her solution. True enough, she didn't have the authority over things to cook on that scale, but Hua Lin did. They would have to work together. Once Hua Lin agreed to go down that path then he belonged to her, there would be no going back for him.

Ms Win-Kham looked sympathetically into Hua Lin's bloodshot and watering eyes.

"I can help you. But from now on only you and I know about this. It has to be our secret."

Hua Lin looked back at her, a little more shocked than he had already been.

"How? How can you help? Do you have fifteen million to lend the bank? That's worth more than ten years of your salary."

"Come now, Hua Lin. Of course I don't have access to that kind of money. But you do. You are the general manager of the Maklai Provincial Bank, after all."

"What? No! I don't have money like that. My salary is

barely double what yours is."

Win-Kham smiled at him like she was indulging a small and innocent child.

"Well of course you don't. But your customers do. How many of them really check the calculations of the interest in their account, understand or even question the various bank charges? Numbers on one ledger can go down or up, depending on who is filling them in, and, more importantly, who is authorising them. The expected number for the cash in the safe will automatically change at the same time."

Hua Lin looked blankly back at her for more explanation. Ms Win-Kham stood up and walked around to his side of the desk. Sitting against the edge of the desk she took his hand.

"We can make the books balance again, but it won't be easy, and it will take time. I can show you what to do and you can authorise it. What you have to understand is now that I'm helping you, we have to work together. We are no longer just colleagues. We are our own team. You and I will share a huge secret that no one else knows, and that means that from here on we have to look after each other."

Hua Lin looked back at her. The gratitude he felt was almost overwhelming. All he knew was that this amazing woman was going to save him from himself. Not for one moment did he suspect he was being played.

Ms Win-Kham produced a number of pages from the folder containing her original cooked documents.

"We need to make a few changes for the bank's costs as well as the accounts of some of the key customers. I suggest we should start with all these new guards you hired. You should officially give them their notice and document that they will finish up at the end of the year, which is about six months away. Meanwhile, we stop them working at the end of the week, and use their future salaries to help start to reduce the missing total."

Hua Lin looked up at her like a helpless puppy. How on earth had things come to this?

"That's all very well, Ms Win-Kham. But it's just a start. It's a drop in the ocean. It's never going to make up for all that missing money."

"Please, call me Win. Now, as you say, it's just a start. One drop of rain you barely notice, but start adding more and more drops and soon there's enough for quite a storm. Let's go through some of the other ways to make up the shortfall. The most obvious is how we calculate monthly interest on some of the bigger accounts. Nobody ever goes back and checks the rates properly. They just accept that we are looking after them. A few very minor reductions on some of the less business-orientated accounts and the gains can be significant."

Hua Lin looked in awe at Ms Win-Kham. She was amazing.

Ms Win-Kham looked back at Mr Hua Lin. He was now complicit in the fraud, which meant that she owned him. He was hers, she had got her very own provincial bank manager. This was the turning point she'd been wanting for for so long. The hard part was done. It would take a while, but once she'd finished putting the accounting straight she would start organising the marriage plans. Of course the marriage would have to take place in Khoyleng where his family was, not in dreary old Maklai. It would be a good opportunity for him to move back to the capital at the same time. Hopefully they would move on a permanent basis.

45. Confession

It was mid-morning when a flustered Mrs Yeo-bo arrived in the office of Mr Tann. Normally, the countenance of Mrs Yeo-bo remained strictly expressionless and without emotion of any kind. This morning was different. She closed the door and turned to face Mr Tann with an expression of agony and panic. Mr Tann looked back at her and gradually developed his own expression of panic, which was reinforced by a sudden feeling of emptiness in the pit of his stomach. It was a bit like being hungry, but without having the need to eat anything. He knew she was good at her job, but how could she have already worked out that he had taken the money from the safe room? He had only done it yesterday evening, towards the end of the working day. At least she had come to him first. That gave him a chance to put things right. After all, he still had all of the money that he'd taken. He could easily claim it was an accident, or perhaps say that he was testing the systems. That was it – it was a test, and she had passed. Mr Tann felt slightly more at ease as he invited her to sit in the chair at the front of his desk.

"Now, Mrs Yeo-bo. You look upset. How can I help you?"

Mrs Yeo-bo looked hard at Mr Tann. Her lower lip

quivered, her face turned red, water swelled in her eyes. She then let out a small yelp, buried her head in her hand and sobbed loudly.

Mr Tann looked at her, horrified, his expression like that of a goat in mid-castration. This was more emotional interaction than he'd ever had with a woman, despite thirty-five years of marriage. If this was the cringeable situation that robbing a bank brought you, then it was definitely not for him. The worst-case scenario he'd imagined was five years in the provincial jail. A quivering woman wailing before him in his office was beyond his worst nightmares.

Mr Tann looked anxiously at the door. He desperately hoped that nobody outside in the corridor could hear any this. What if someone came in to see what was going on, and found him alone with a female cashier in his room – being 'emotional'. Mr Tann quickly walked over to the door and slid the bolt across. This was no time for unnecessary interruptions.

"Mrs Yeo-bo. Whatever is the matter with you? This is most unusual. This is not the kind of outburst I would expect from a respectable member of the staff like yourself."

Mr Tann produced a silk handkerchief from his jacket pocket and passed it to her. She gratefully took it and blew her nose into it with considerable force and volume before handing it back. Mr Tann dropped it straight into the bin behind his desk and began looking for something to wipe his own hand with. Eventually he grabbed a few sheets of blank deposit forms and scrunched them up into a ball, rubbing his hands on them as he did so. He then sat back at his desk and waited for Mrs Yeo-bo to get her emotions under control. Supplying a handkerchief had been the only reasonable solution he could come up with, but it seemed to have had little effect.

Eventually Mrs Yeo-bo looked up from her hands, her eyes were red and blurry.

"Mr Tann, they've checked the cash three times this morning. Three times! He's had Ms Win-Kham counting all the money. Three times she's checked now. Oh, what have I done?!"

The word 'done' tailed off into a further screech, which itself tailed off into more sobbing. Mr Tann once more decided to just sit and wait things out until the latest bout of unsolicited emotion had run its course. Eventually the uncomfortable disturbance quietened to a slightly more reserved series of sniffles. After the initial shock of the woman's arrival, a more thoughtful Mr Tann took a different tack on the conversation:

"What is it that you think you have done, Mrs Yeo-bo?"

Mrs Yeo-bo took a moment to try to compose herself.

"I've been taking money from the bank. I've been doing it for years. As a cashier, I've been able to change the books to cover it up. And now they've found out!"

Mrs Yeo-bo was about to leap into another fit of hysteria when Mr Tann reached forward and took her hand. He rather surprised himself in this, but he couldn't face a third round of unfettered emotion.

"Perhaps you need to calm down, Mrs Yeo-bo. We've known each other a very long time. Let's go through the problem slowly and see if there is a way we can sort this out."

Mr Tann couldn't believe his luck. His tired and haggard slouch brought on by years of dogged service and a night of designing safe room plans with his annoyingly smug brother-in-law was immediately replaced by a youthful and jaunty countenance. He was the one that had stolen the money the day before and now someone else was admitting to long-term theft from the bank.

Mrs Yeo-bo had chosen a remarkably well-timed day for her confession to Mr Tann. A few months ago, a situation like this would have brought out the moral authoritarian in Mr Tann. He would have demanded an enquiry and marched her down to the police station himself. Recently though, he'd started to see things as a little bit less black and white.

Mrs Yeo-bo nodded in a pleading sort of way.

"I'll pay it back, I just need some time. I shouldn't have done it, but I needed the extra to put our girl through school. My salary wasn't enough, and Mr Yeo-bo would drink and gamble away any money he'd got from the factory. Not that he ever had much. He's a useless man really. It was my parents that were determined we should marry. Anyway, he went off with another woman and has not been back in the last two years. Not that it makes much difference to the bills, but it was that much harder to pay my daughter's school fees. I will pay it back, I promise. Just please give me a second chance."

Mr Tann pondered for a while over the options. If Hua Lin was demanding the cash counts, three of them in one morning, then he must have found a problem with the ledgers or the cash. This still looked bad for Mr Tann, despite his colleague's confession. They might add up what she was confessing to and realise they were still short.

"You can stay in here in my office until you feel a bit better, Mrs Yeo-bo. Then maybe you should go home on sick leave for the day. Actually, maybe take the rest of the week, just to be sure. I'll see what I can find out from Mr Hua Lin and let you know what is concerning him."

Mrs Yeo-bo sniffled loudly.

"And also, Mrs Yeo-bo. Don't think that this is necessarily an end to the matter. There may be consequences. Please don't leave town, and when things are clearer I will follow up on this issue."

With that, Mr Tann invited Mrs Yeo-bo to depart from his room. He felt fairly terrible about his closing remarks but he couldn't have Mrs Yeo-bo thinking he had something to hide as well. He couldn't be seen to be too keen to tidy up her indiscretions.

46. Investigation

It was shortly before midday that Mr Tann knocked confidently on the door of Mr Hua Lin and let himself into the manager's office. He had kept the door of his own office ajar so that he could monitor the comings and goings of Mr Hua Lin's engagements. The original appointment with his boss had been for eleven, but Mr Tann could see that the events of the morning outside of his room had taken over any predetermined scheduling that might exist. It had been about fifteen minutes since Ms Win-Kham had finally left Hua Lin's office, and he decided the time was ripe to do some investigating of his own. It was like the meeting of two men who had swapped their bodies in a bizarre science experiment. Mr Tann arrived brimming with confidence and with a positive spring in his step, whilst Mr Hua Lin slouched over his desk with the air of a defeated man who was about to crumble before him.

"Good morning, Mr Hua Lin! I wonder if now is a good time to discuss those security measures for the safe room. I've had some designs prepared. Perhaps you would be good enough to take a look and see if you approve of what I've had drawn up?"

With that, Mr Tann unrolled his document and spread it on the table in front of Hua Lin. This had two effects.

Firstly, Hua Lin seemed to completely lose what little colour had remained in his face, brought on by the realisation that Mr Tann's recent focus on a lack of safe room security compounded the difficult situation he was in, and that was strongly linked to poor safe room security. The second effect was that Mr Tann could cast his well-seasoned financial eye over the other documents that were spread haphazardly across the table. It did indeed look as though Mr Hua Lin was retracing transactions and reviewing the ledger records for the past few years in considerable detail. It was an exercise which was clearly causing him a huge amount of stress.

"What do you think then, Mr Hua Lin?"

Mr Tann continued with his jaunty approach and pretended not to see the disaster that he had clearly interrupted.

"The idea is that we get a new safe, around four times the current capacity, and install it in that corner over there. That way we can bring it in through the front double doors, knock through part of the wall there, bolt it down and then rebuild the wall. There would be a new security door here with a password keypad, and then the old safe would be brought behind the counters and used to manage the day to day money for the cashiers."

Mr Tann felt quite smug with himself. Not only had he actually taken command of the safe room assignment, but clearly the whole thing was making Hua Lin extremely uncomfortable.

"Well it sounds very good, Mr Tann. Perhaps you can get the project started and liaise with head office on what you need."

Mr Tann noticed that Hua Lin had said all of that without either looking up from the ledgers that were absorbing his attention, or even glancing at the plans.

"Very good, Mr Hua Lin. I take it that I have your approval then. I'll start this afternoon. If I may say, you seem rather preoccupied with something. Is there anything at all I can help you with?"

Hua Lin looked up at Mr Tann with his gaunt eyes."

"No, nothing in particular. I'm just making a thorough check of the books. I've decided I should do this every month. It's good to be diligent about these things."

"Very good, Mr Hua Lin. It seems to be a very wise precaution."

With that Mr Tann gathered up his safe room design and let himself out of the office.

***

Back behind the sanctity of his own desk, Mr Tann was able to analyse the situation. The facts were these: firstly he had stolen a small amount of money, and seemed to have got away with it. Secondly, Mrs Yeo-bo had confessed, but only to him, that she'd been skimming a few notes on a regular basis to pay for her kid's schooling. Thirdly, Ms Win-Kham and Mr Hua Lin had been in cahoots all morning investigating the books. The last fact was the one that didn't quite fit. If Ms Win-Kham had spotted that the money was missing from the previous night, then Hua Lin didn't need to spend hours of research to work out that one problem. If they'd found out about Mrs Yeo-bo's fraudulent activity, then it would also be quickly apparent who was at fault. Mrs Yeo-bo would have been hauled into the manager's office where Hua Lin would have demanded an explanation. It would not be something that demanded a lot of cloak and dagger escapades and collusion with Ms Win-Kham. In fact, it would be something that would be brought to Mr Tann's attention and managed through the proper channels. An ongoing problem stretching back over a couple of years would certainly not be something for Mr Hua Lin to worry about. It wasn't done on his watch, and indeed it was following his recent arrival that the problem had been found. His reputation was quite safe, if not bolstered by this discovery. Meanwhile, he had the demeanour and pallor of someone on the brink of a nervous breakdown. It didn't add up at all.

Mr Tann might have been getting a bit older and a bit slower, but he was not stupid. There was clearly far more to the goings on at the bank that day than he immediately knew. It was clear to him that the problems in the bank were far bigger than he was currently party to, that Hua Lin was somehow more culpable than he realised, and that Ms Win-Kham was playing it for all she was worth.

Mr Tann had been subjected to a very strange dream the previous night. He'd not got much sleep in between the need to make a safe room design with his brother-in-law and the time needed to lie awake worrying about it. However, for the small period when he had drifted off, the oddest series of visions had come to him and had stuck with him long after he awoke. As he cast his mind back to the memory, it was as if there had been a deep forest, and in the depths of the undergrowth a spirit resembling Old Papa Han had emerged from behind a large tree. Or maybe he was the tree. It was difficult to tell with dreams, they were always so difficult to remember with proper clarity. What he could recall was how smug that tree spirit had somehow managed to look, certainly far more smug than a tree can usually conjure up. He wasn't sure how he knew that the tree was Papa Han, or even that it was smug, but it seemed to be telling him that everything was going to be okay.

47. The Post-Heist Shift

Kheng had been very much on alert during his first post-heist shift. The day after the heist was, after all, the time when he and his band of thieves were most likely to get rumbled. Especially if it turned out that the bank had the systems in place to spot that they were missing a few sacks of cash.

By the time he arrived for the afternoon shift, Kheng was relieved to see that all was still well. Superficially at least. Customers continued to come and go. There was no undue presence of swarms of police or army personnel to cart him away to some grim detention centre. Nobody from management had called the guards into the manager's office to ask whether they had suspected the presence of intruders during the night. However, despite the comfortable sense of predictable routine, it still didn't quite seem like a completely normal day.

The first anomaly had been explained to him by Meebor shortly after he arrived for his shift. Meebor told him that, at around ten o'clock that morning, he had witnessed the unexpected departure of Mrs Yeo-bo the cashier. He'd said good morning as she approached the gates to leave the compound, but there was no pleasantry or acknowledgment in reply. Meebor reckoned that she looked about ten years older than when he had seen her earlier in the week. She always appeared a bit older than she really was as she dressed so formally, and always had her hair in a tight bun that was so symmetrical it looked almost unreal. However, Meebor had observed that the Mrs Yeo-bo that was departing this morning had a few hairs straggling to the side of the once immaculate coiffure. The tucking in of her blouse was missing its usual military precision, her usual perfectly made up facade now looked lined and tired, the once emotionless eyes were now a window flung open to reveal a tormented soul. Kheng was almost on the brink of being shocked by this news. Such a day-to-day contrast of character was rare amongst the bank's administrative employees.

The end of the opening hours that afternoon brought a new wave of unusual sights. Mr Tann was the first to leave the bank. In the past, Kheng would never have described Mr Tann as 'jaunty'. Kheng was far too respectful, and Mr Tann had never chosen to display any degree of jauntiness about him. However, were there ever to be a day when a primordial need had overcome all reason and the label of 'jaunty' needed to be applied, then this was the moment to grasp at it. The head clerk departed from the front door's step with the agility of a grasshopper and the contentment of a small boy who was aware of his growing reputation in the discipline of marbles. The contrasting image between the enveloping dark storm that had consumed Mrs Yeo-bo and the springtime meadow breeze that wafted Mr Tann through the bank's gates and down the street was both striking and confusing.

Of equal note was the departure of Mr Hua Lin and Ms Win-Kham. Or rather, the lack thereof. Both were busy in the office for over an hour after the bank should have been closed. This was unheard of in Maklai banking terms. The hours were set for work and they were either followed or skived from. To do extra would only raise suspicion. It certainly raised Kheng's suspicion. He made several rounds of the bank's perimeter so that he could peer through the windows to see what was going on. Mainly it was paperwork. Both of them were in Hua Lin's office surrounded by bank documents and examining each one of them with a high degree of diligence. Kheng had at first wondered if they were investigating the robbery, but soon dismissed the idea. If they had discovered the missing money then they would have to call for the police, and then head office. The guards would have been the first ones dragged inside for questioning. Mr Hua Lin was many things, but one of those was a man who followed the rule book and procedures to the letter. Kheng's back up theory for the sudden change in behaviour was that the two of them were having an affair. Nelea, Kheng's wife, would be delighted if that was the case as Kheng never had good gossip for her to shock Mama Tae with. Being the first one to know about this kind of scandal in their small provincial town would temporarily send her to film star status. At least for a day or so until everyone got bored with it and some other scandalous revelation turned up. So it was all a bit odd and, despite the lack of dramatic police arrivals, it made Kheng feel nervous.

When eventually both Hua Lin and Win-Kham departed, Kheng was able to take note of their demeanour. Ms Win-Kham was looking pleased with herself. Very pleased. She was energetic and had a light in her face that Kheng had never noticed before. She was not at all tired for her long day's work or resentful at having to stay late in the office. Kheng felt happy for her. He'd always worried that she looked so uninspired, like her life was being slowly wasted, as she drudged through her working routine. Mr

Hua Lin, meanwhile, looked relieved. He looked tired as well, but mostly gave off an aura of relief, as if a great burden had been lifted from him. Neither of these was an emotion that was compatible with those of people who had just uncovered evidence of a daring bank heist.

As they walked through the gate and took turns to balance across the planks that traversed the entrenched footpath, Hua Lin offered to walk Ms Win-Kham to a restaurant for dinner. He explained that it would be only fair of him as he'd kept her late from returning home and being able to cook for herself. She politely accepted, and life and energy seemed to glow from her face even more.

Kheng locked the gates and sat down on the faded old plastic chair. He was a little envious that his colleagues would be going to the restaurant. Unusually, he'd decided to bring his evening meal to work with him. What with all of the other goings on in the past twenty-four hours, he'd concluded that risking the wall-climb and having his dinner break back at the house might be pushing his luck a little too far. It was now a whole working day since the bank heist had been carried out. No one had called the police, no one had sent for the guards to explain possible break-ins, nobody had arrived from head office to initiate a formal investigation. Maybe, just maybe, the mischievous tree spirit of the late Papa Han had helped them through, and they had got away with it. Sure, there had been a few odd goings-on that day. But a few odd goings on was not really that unusual for Maklai. Even when everything was normal it was still a little bit odd.

48. Hospital

Three weeks later..

Kheng sat in the waiting area at the front of Maklai Provincial Hospital. Before him in the opposite wall was a small hatch with a sliding piece of glass, behind which, one of the administrative staff was busying herself with a pile of official-looking forms. About ten other people were waiting there next to him, sitting in the row of grubby plastic chairs. One of them had crutches and a plaster-cast, for the others it was hard to tell if they were there as patients or visitors. Some were probably relatives of patients waiting to see how they were faring, or to bring them food. All of them were staring at the old TV that was hanging from the ceiling in a sturdy metal cage of welded square bars above the receptionist's window, captivated by a cheap soap opera that was delivering some amateur dramatics of unrequited love. The cage looked too heavy to remain so securely attached to the ceiling and was probably worth more than the TV. Next to the receptionist's window was the counter for the pharmacist, who was sorting through a box filled with coloured pills in small plastic bags. To his right was a doctor's consultation room. Through the open door he could see there was a young guy having a wound treated on his leg. A big bottle of brown liquid was being sponged liberally onto the oozing graze with a ball of cotton wool. The kid had no doubt fallen off his motorbike. He probably came off trying to impress either a girl or some of the bigger kids. Kheng was glad that he was no longer under pressure to impress others in the way that he had felt when he was the same age as that kid. The doctor's corner of the hospital looked whiter and more hygienic than where he sat with his queue of soap opera devotees. However, the hospital block was an old concrete building that had been built to be very open, to try to keep it cool. It was suffering from its aging construction and a limited budget. Kheng admired how the staff managed to maintain such pockets of hygiene to ensure that the patients were looked after where it really counted. From where Kheng sat he could see into the corner of the doctor's room. There was a wooden cupboard with a glass door. It was crammed high with old documents, presumably for patients who no longer had need of them. Looking through the glass door they seemed orderly enough. After a while, Kheng noticed that the base of the cupboard had given way under the weight of the aging hospital records. In the small gap between the floor and cupboard was where the stack of mouse-chewed paperwork started, still sitting on the plywood from inside the cupboard. It was a bit like the bank really. It appeared normal and orderly enough from an initial inspection, but stare too long and the quirks and abnormalities would surface soon enough.

Kheng turned his attention to the TV, having exhausted the other points of interest in his immediate vision. As he did so, he saw Mr Salt walking down the corridor towards him.

"Mr Kheng. I'm so glad you came."

Kheng offered up the small plastic bag of fruit that he had put on the floor under his chair.

"I picked up some fruit."

Mr Salt kindly observed the bag.

"Rambutans. She'll enjoy them."

"How is your wife? Did everything go well?"

"It's okay now, Kheng. I came in early this morning to check on her after the operation."

"What about those expensive machines that she needed?"

"It was all organised with the doctor days ago. She's already getting all of the treatment. I told him I would pay up-front for the main treatment and so he arranged it with the administration. I then have to make smaller weekly payments to cover anything extra. I'm supposed to sort out the next payment today, in fact. The administrator is in the next building. First though, you should meet my wife. She'd really appreciate seeing you. She's just down the corridor in one of the wards there on the left. The kids are with her."

"Yes. Of course. I'd be very happy to see how she's doing."

Mr Salt beamed at Kheng as if lots of happiness was trying to show itself all at once but his face wasn't used to the exertion. Kheng assumed that the additional joy was partly due to the Salts' children being there. He got the impression that for Mr Salt's son to engage enthusiastically would have been victory enough on any day, regardless of the circumstances.

Kheng wasn't particularly comfortable when meeting ill people. He didn't really know what he was supposed to say. 'How are you?' he would ask. They would then politely say they were 'not so bad', and meanwhile everyone knew that they were really feeling awful and asking probably hadn't helped. Should he then be upbeat and chatty to try to inject some positivity into the atmosphere, or was it more appropriate to remain demure and respectful? It was so hard to tell.

In the ward, Mr Salt's son and daughter were sitting quietly next to the bed looking demure. Kheng decided that as the mood was already set, it wouldn't do to deviate too much. He stepped up next to the bed and put the fruit on the table at the side.

"Hello. I'm a friend of your husband's. We worked together at the bank."

She smiled back at him.

"I've heard all about you from Salt. I think we have a lot to thank you for, Mr Kheng."

Kheng smiled back.

"I'm always happy to help out a friend."

"Well, if you hadn't told Salt all about that dream of yours he would never have put his salary on the lottery numbers and won all that money. Lucky I was stuck in here at the time or I'd have never let him do it."

Kheng looked over at Mr Salt. Salt looked straight back at him with a firm expression. It suggested that, in light of all that had gone on in recent weeks, this final small distortion of honesty was hardly here or there. Kheng gave an almost undetectable nod.

"...'cause, normally I'd batter his ears for wasting our money on lottery games like that when we're so strapped for cash. However, I guess I'll let it go this time. What a fantastic dream though, Mr Kheng. Especially as it was so lucky with the numbers. Maybe there's more to it than just the lottery?"

Kheng tried to look as though he was giving this suggestion some thought.

"Maybe there is. We could ask my neighbour, Mama Tae. She seems to be interested in other worldly goings on. You know, hearing the words of tree spirits, analysing strange events, the meaning of dreams and that sort of thing."

Kheng turned to Mr Salt:

"Are you coming this afternoon? It's the big party at the bank. I've been put in charge of some of the entertainment by Mr Tann."

"I'd not forgotten, Mr Kheng. Looking forward to it. After all, there's quite a lot to celebrate."

49. Fireworks

The firecrackers exploded into life and then several ear-rattling rockets shot up into the air. Kheng moved back and sat on his plastic chair at a safe distance at the side of the bank's compound, so that he could admire his creation.

He had had considerable time to prepare the firework display and so had planned the entire extravaganza in meticulous detail. The first wooden post that was laden with rockets and firecrackers was positioned just to the side of the main gate. Kheng had waited for the end of Mr Tann's speech and then ceremoniously lit the fuse. The crackers were loud, maybe louder than the ones at Papa Han's funeral. The rockets then shot upwards, some of them less upwards, some of them not upwards at all. This was not unexpected by the gathering of invited guests, who would duck whilst remaining in awe at the ferocity of the display. As the firecrackers burned down the post, the fuse was lit on a rocket that was connected to a wire. The rocket shot forward and was guided upward to an even bigger stash of rockets and firecrackers on the roof that had been set up by Kheng earlier that morning. The crowd looked on at the display, which continued its haphazard explosion of fun and near-misses. Kheng was a methodical person and could easily have set up the whole thing to make sure that all the rockets went skywards, but he was not so old and sensible as to want to take all of the excitement out of the event. What wasn't so clear to the crowd from below was the way that two future rockets had been set up with wires and were specifically aimed at the two security cameras which continued to spy on the front gates and door of the bank. Kheng observed as his two carefully designed rockets took it in turns to obliterate, in spectacular fashion, each of the cameras on the front of the building. No one else noticed as they were too busy focusing on the need to dodge other stray rockets.

Kheng smiled. He'd been saving his rockets for his own funeral. However, he had decided it would be nicer to use them to celebrate life as it was happening, not after it was gone. Besides, if Papa Han could be a mischievous old tree spirit in his next life then there was every chance that Kheng would be blessed with his dream of becoming a bird flying above the forests. Maybe he'd even nest somewhere near Old Papa Han.

At the back of the compound, Mr Tann was pouring more drinks for his guests and chatting with the men in suits that had come down from head office. He looked happy. He was happy. Maybe the promotion of Mr Tann to manager of the bank was the ultimate aim of Papa Han when he started interfering with Kheng's dreaming. The robbery was somehow the catalyst for all of the subsequent changes, and now Mr Tann was succeeding Papa Han. He guessed that was what the old man had always intended.

50. Night Guard

By 4.00pm most of the guests had left the bank. The party was over and Mr Tann was undisputed as the new manager of the Maklai Provincial Bank.

More than two weeks had passed since the night of the bank heist. There had been a lot of changes since then. A lot.

The most striking event had been the return of Mr Hua Lin to Khoyleng. It had taken a couple of weeks, but it seemed that he was desperate to return to his old but less exalted life in the big city. To many people's surprise he proposed to Ms Win-Kham and took her back to Khoyleng with him.

Mr Hua Lin's last day as the provincial manager had been a fairly predictable affair. The morning had seen a notable change of routine as the various banking staff looked for opportunities to go into the manager's office, express their regret at his sudden departure, and provide a small leaving present, usually a gift basket from the market containing various essentials like jars of honey, toothpaste, and packs of biscuits. For senior staff, the essential sign of respect was to include some local spirit or whisky within the offerings.

Before his departure Hua Lin had stopped the contracts

of both Meebor and Salt with an apology and an early salary payment that covered the first month. The relief guard position was cancelled before it had even started. The bank was back to one guard, and Kheng was back to the old routine. He would start his shift when Mr Tann locked up for the evening and finish when he arrived in the morning. It was a system that had always suited Kheng just fine. Kheng suspected that the sudden 'cut backs' in staff at the bank were strongly linked to an awareness within the management of some missing finances. So did the other two guards, which is why they didn't protest too strongly when they were given their swift notice. Besides, they both had sufficient wealth, and no longer needed the work.

Kheng tidied up some of the discarded rubbish that was scattered near to the gate. He then seated himself in the faded plastic chair at the front of the office and surveyed. The storm drain had finally been covered over, a path with paving stones had been laid on top. Even proper man-hole covers had been installed over the gaps in the pipe. It would now be very difficult to climb down in there and sneak off for dinner, but that didn't really matter any more. Eventually, Mr Tann locked up the kitchen at the back of the bank, which had been the hub of the party catering, and made his way past Kheng and out to the street. He thanked Kheng for organising the fireworks as he did so. He even made a remark about the weather, without being prompted by Kheng to make conversation. It was as though the world would never be the same again. Kheng felt that Mr Tann appeared to be physically a lot healthier these days. Happier in a way, less slouched perhaps. Having never previously given the impression of being happy then it was probably quite difficult for him to start at his age. However, he did seem to have a little more verve than his usual pottering suggested, which could only be for the good.

It was like Mama Tae had implied when he'd told her about all of the sudden changes in staff at the bank. Sometimes it looks like things are changing because everything is different for a while. It's only really a change if you can look back a long way and no longer recognise where you've come from. Normally Mama Tae was a bit obscure, and years of hitting the rice wine early on in the day had probably played quite a big part in that. However, on this occasion, her disjointed rambling had been quite astute.

Kheng looked to the back of the compound and at the sun setting behind the old jackfruit tree. It would be dark soon. Good. He'd be able to slip out through the gates and pop back home to get his dinner.

www.ingramcontent.com/pod-product-compliance
Lightning Source LLC
Chambersburg PA
CBHW032210190626
46810CB00019B/2421